MAGIC & MYTHOS

STARRY HOLLOW WITCHES, BOOK 8

ANNABEL CHASE

RED PALM PRESS LLC

CHAPTER ONE

THE CEILING FAN whirred above my head. I watched each blade as it passed the small crack in the ceiling. *Thirty-one. Thirty-two.* I only wanted to focus on the movement of the fan. Nothing else. Life was easier this way.

"Mom?"

"In here," I called weakly.

Marley appeared in the doorway. She frowned when she saw me sprawled across the bed. "Are you sick?"

"Sort of."

She sighed and crawled into bed beside me. "You can't keep going like this."

"You underestimate my abilities," I replied.

My daughter laughed softly. "I wouldn't dare."

I flipped onto my side to face her. "This is what guilt looks like, Marley. Take a good, hard look, so you don't ever have to subject yourself to it."

"Get a grip. You didn't kill anyone," she insisted. "You listened to your heart. Finally."

I wrapped an arm around her. I didn't want to talk about it anymore. It had been three days since I broke up with

Sheriff Nash and I still felt terrible for hurting him. Since then, a tight ball of guilt had lodged in my chest and refused to budge.

"I think I need a healer," I said. "Maybe we should call Cephas."

"What you need is a kick in the pants," Marley replied. "You made a tough decision and now you have to live with the consequences, but the bright side is that you made the choice. No one made it for you. It's much harder to suffer the consequences when you didn't play a role in the decision, like when Dad died."

I squinted at her. "Are you sure you're only eleven?"

"What can I say? I inherited your deep well of wisdom."

I laughed in her face. "It's a deep well of something. Not sure we can call what I have wisdom." I rolled onto my back. "You need to get ready for school. Can't have you showing up late on your last day." Now that Marley had come into her magic, Aunt Hyacinth had wasted no time in registering her at the exclusive Black Cloak Academy.

"If you need me, I'll stay here."

My heart squeezed. How did I get so lucky? "I'm an adult, most of the time. It's not your job to worry about me. How are you feeling about your last day?" A little deflection never hurt anybody.

"My friends are sad I'm leaving, of course, but I'll only be right down the street." She beamed. "I can't wait until orientation."

"Don't you think it will be strange to only have classes with witches and wizards?" I asked.

She laughed. "Don't you think it was strange to have classes with *any* paranormals when we first came here? My New Jersey school had plenty of weirdos, but no vampires or werewolves." Normally, a move to a new town and a new school would throw a kid for a loop. Not Marley. The transition to life in Starry Hollow had been a positive experience for her and, for that, I was grateful.

"Fair point, but at least there's diversity in the public school here." Marley was friends with elves, fairies, vampires —at the academy, she'd only develop close bonds with para-normals like her. We'd need to make an effort to expand her friendship circle. I didn't want her growing up in an echo chamber.

"The upside is I won't have to be you, Mom," she said.

"Gee, thanks. Way to kick me when I'm down."

She giggled. "You know what I mean. Grown up and learning magic for the first time. The academy will make sure I know how to use magic responsibly from a young age."

I gave her a pointed look. "Are you suggesting I'm not responsible?"

"I'm suggesting that you missed out on not going to magic school, that's all."

"I missed out on a lot more than that, you know." A mother. A sense of family.

She nestled in the crook of my arm. "I know. I'm sorry. I wasn't trying to be difficult. That's at least two more years away."

I jabbed her gently with my elbow. "Very funny. You will not be a typical teenager, Marley. Promise me right now."

"I promise. I'll save my moodiness for when I go away to college and then I'll have no friends."

I patted my chest. "Hey, there isn't room for any more guilt in here. Stop where you are."

Don't worry. I'll keep her in line, a voice said. Raoul, my raccoon familiar, stuck his head out of a drawer. He quickly snatched a pair of my pajama bottoms off his head.

I bolted upright. "Sweet baby Elvis. How long have you been there?"

I fell asleep. It was so cozy in there.

"In my pajama drawer?"

Reluctantly, he left the comfort of the drawer and scampered over to the bed. *Your ugly crying needs work, by the way. The grimace isn't quite where it needs to be, but we can work on it.*

You weren't supposed to be watching me like a creeper, I told him.

I'm concerned, he replied. *I'm your familiar. I can tell when you're upset.*

Then let me know you're here for me instead of hiding in a drawer. It's bizarre and very unwelcome.

So ungrateful, he muttered.

"Would you mind taking PP3 out for a walk before school?" I asked Marley. "I haven't been downstairs yet and I heard him jump off the bed a little while ago." Our Yorkshire terrier, Prescott Peabody III, was getting up there in years, so he wasn't as desperate for outside time as he used to be. He took so long to poop these days that I felt the desire to bring him a newspaper and a cup of coffee.

"Sure, Mom. No problem." Marley failed to make a move.

"What?" I prompted.

She chewed her lip. "I was just wondering…It's been a few days and I'm sure Alec has heard the news by now. Have you talked to him since you broke up with the sheriff?"

A groan rumbled inside me. "Not yet." I knew he was giving me space. He'd shown up in my bedroom the other night and blew up my world. My neat and tidy world where I dated the loyal and emotionally available werewolf Granger Nash. In a shocking turn of events, the vampire admitted his feelings for me and claimed he was ready to move forward with our relationship. Like the ceiling fan, my world hadn't stopped spinning since then. So far, I'd successfully avoided the *Vox Populi* office where he was the editor-in-chief and I worked as a fledgling reporter.

"You are going to date him, aren't you?" she asked. "I hope

this isn't going to be one of those choosing yourself moments because you've been alone long enough."

"I'm not alone," I objected. "I have you and PP3."

And me, Raoul added.

Not all company is created equal, I said.

Hey! Watch your tongue or I'll spend the next few hours in your underwear drawer.

I wrinkled my nose in disgust.

"You know what I mean," Marley said. "If you broke up with Sheriff Nash because of Alec, then you need to give him a real chance. Otherwise, what's the point?"

I shifted back to face the ceiling fan again. "I broke up with the sheriff because of *me*, but yes—to answer your question—I'm giving him a chance." That was the reason I'd broken up with the sheriff the very same night Alec came to see me. I knew I couldn't string him along for another second. He deserved better. That didn't stop me from feeling sick over it, though. I had feelings for Granger, that much was true. They just weren't as powerful as what I felt for Alec. If there was a chance we could make it work, I owed it to myself to try.

"Make sure you have magic lessons today," Marley said. "Don't cancel. You need to stay active."

"Yes, Mom," I said in a mock bored tone. "And I'm going to work, too. It's time to get the circulation flowing again." I'd cancelled my previous lessons without explanation. I didn't need the whole town gossiping, though I knew they probably were anyway.

Marley kissed my cheek. "I'm proud of you, Mom."

I blinked at her. "You are? Why?" I'd crushed a good werewolf's heart after finally agreeing to date him. I didn't deserve praise. I deserved a bowl of spaghetti over the head.

"I think what you did was brave," she replied. "I know it doesn't seem that way."

5

"No, it doesn't at all. It seems selfish and foolish." Alec would likely change his mind after three weeks and I'd have thrown away any hope of a healthy relationship with Granger.

"Trust your gut," Marley said. "Isn't that what you always tell me? You had instincts about Alec, that there's a decent vampire lurking underneath the cool exterior. He's just not as obvious about his goodness as the sheriff. It's like he's ashamed of it or something. There's a story there."

"He's a vampire," I said. "I suspect there are lots of stories there." He wasn't born emotionally unavailable. Something happened to make him that way. That was something I'd been thinking a lot about during my special time with the ceiling fan. How could I start us off on the right path so that he didn't shut down when we hit a rough patch, as we inevitably would?

A bark from downstairs interrupted us.

"I think PP3 has reached the limits of his patience." Marley rolled off the bed. "Try to have a great day, okay?"

"I will."

Liar, Raoul said.

I glared at the raccoon as I called after Marley, "I hope it's a fabulous last day!" It seemed that Marley and I were both crossing a threshold this week. At least hers didn't involve destroying anyone's soul, unless you counted her English teacher, who'd surely miss Marley's clever insights.

Please tell me you're going to shower today, Raoul said. *This room smells like a football locker room after the Super Bowl*. He inhaled deeply. *Not that I mind*.

"You're disgusting." I flipped back the covers and hurried to the bathroom to shower off the stench. Only when I closed the door did I hear the faint laughter of my familiar.

CHAPTER TWO

"WELL, well, well. Look what the ill wind blew in." Bentley Smith observed me with interest as I shuffled from the door to my desk at *Vox Populi*.

"It's good to see you, Ember," Tanya said. "We were starting to worry."

"I think 'we' is overstating it slightly," Bentley said.

"Sorry that I haven't been here," I said. "There's been a lot going on."

"Same here. I was hoping you'd both be in today because I have news," Tanya said. The office manager came fluttering over to my desk.

"So do I," I said. I wasn't sure how much of my news to share. Probably best to limit it to the sheriff. Alec guarded his privacy like a dragon with treasure.

"Me first," Bentley said, shooting up from his seat. "I've been waiting all morning."

My gaze shifted to the clock on the wall. "An entire hour, Bentley? How ever have you managed?" I cast a glance at Tanya. "Man, I'd hate to be his parents on Christmas morning." Or any morning, really.

7

Bentley broke into a broad smile. "Meadow and I are engaged."

I gaped at the elf. "Wow. Like to be married?"

"No, we're engaged in a riveting game of Dungeons & Dragons," he huffed. "Yes, of course to be married."

"That's wonderful, Bentley." Tanya zoomed over to him to offer a motherly hug. "Meadow is absolutely lovely. I'm delighted for you both."

"You're very lucky," I said. "Meadow is a catch. When's the big day?"

"It's still under discussion," he replied. "Meadow has a few difficult family members and…"

I held up my hand. "Okay, I don't need all the details. My news is pressing."

Bentley folded his arms. "What a surprise. Sixty seconds of Bentley. Now I suppose it's sixty minutes of Ember."

I dropped into the chair beside him. "Fine. I won't tell you."

Tanya clasped her hands together, her wings fluttering madly. "My news *is* rather pressing, so I should probably just blurt it out. My niece is back in town."

At first I didn't understand the implication. "That's nice. Is she staying with you?"

Tanya cocked her head at me. "Unfortunately, she is. I'm hoping it's only a brief visit. She's apparently been named the beneficiary in a will and she's come to claim it. Money is about the only thing that girl responds to."

"I can think of something besides money," Bentley muttered.

"What's with the weird vibe?" I asked, looking from Bentley to Tanya. "We all have annoying family members we have to suffer through. At least yours doesn't live at the end of your driveway."

"I think it's safe to say there's a comfortable distance

between Rose Cottage and Thornhold," Bentley pointed out. "The estate isn't exactly quaint."

No, Thornhold was massive and I could go weeks without seeing anyone if I planned my day right. Of course, Aunt Hyacinth would demand my presence at Sunday dinner, and it would be difficult to hide if she came searching for me.

Tanya tapped her finger pads together. "Oh, dear. I hate to be the one to remind you, Ember, but my niece is Tatiana." The fairy waited expectantly.

"Okay," I said slowly.

"Oh, for gods' sake," Bentley said, tossing a pen over his shoulder in frustration. "Tatiana is the fairy that broke the hearts of both of your illustrious suitors. The reason they despise each other."

Tanya held up a finger. "To be fair, werewolves and vampires have a long history of difficult relations."

My head was spinning as the information sunk in. *That* Tatiana.

"Does Alec know?" Bentley asked.

"I don't believe so," Tanya said. "She only darkened my doorstep last evening, without warning, I might add. A little notice would've been nice. I'd just settled down with a book and a cup of wistberry tea."

"Well, your news is more interesting than I expected," I said. I thought she was going to produce a scarf she knitted without a pattern or something equally snore-inducing.

Tanya smiled at the compliment. "Thank you."

My brain was still fuzzy. Tatiana had pitted Alec and Granger against each other and then broke both their hearts by leaving town with a centaur. Of course, she'd used more than her feminine wiles to do it—she'd used magic. This was not great timing, especially under the circumstances.

Before I could ask more questions, the front door opened

and Alec breezed in. Whistling. The stoic vampire was whistling. Although he wore one of his expensive custom suits, there was a casual air to his presence. Even his blond hair wasn't as slick as usual. It looked soft and inviting and I fought the urge to scurry over and run my fingers through it. He must've heard the news about the sheriff.

I wasn't the only one to notice the change in demeanor. Bentley and Tanya stared at him, unsure what to think of their relaxed boss. Had he avoided the office the last few days, too?

"Good morning, Alec," Tanya said. "I hope your days off were productive. Can I get you anything?"

Alec greeted her with a smile. "Not today, Tanya. I have everything I need." He looked at me and winked. "Don't I, Miss Rose?"

I gulped. I thought we'd play it cool. Apparently not.

Now it was Bentley and Tanya's turn to stare at me.

"I'll be in my office," Alec said. "I have a call in twenty minutes, so I would appreciate no interruptions." He strode back to his private office with a spring in his step. The undead seemed to have come back to life.

My colleagues waited until they heard the soft click of his door to turn on me. "What was that all about?" Bentley asked. If his eyes grew any bigger, I worried they'd pop out of their sockets.

I shrugged and turned on my computer. "I told you I had news. You weren't interested."

Bentley jumped out of his chair and smacked his hands on the corner of my desk. "I take it all back. I'm more than happy to endure sixty minutes of All About Ember."

I kept my gaze fixed on my screen. "I'll bet you are."

Tanya clapped her hands together. "I have no idea what the details are, but I feel extremely pleased with this development."

Bentley turned to look at her. "I thought you liked Sheriff Nash."

"Oh, I absolutely do, but Alec is family," Tanya replied. "You always want the best for your family." She frowned. "Even the ones that make life challenging."

Bentley peered at me. "So you dumped the sheriff? Does this mean I'll be able to accompany him on investigations now?"

I laughed. "*That's* your concern?"

He straightened. "It's not a concern. Just thinking out loud."

I groaned. "You're so transparent, Bentley. You may as well be made of glass."

"What happened then?" Tanya asked. "I thought you and the sheriff were officially an item."

My throat tightened as I remembered the pained expression on Granger's face when I ended things. It was excruciating. I nearly changed my mind at the last second, but I knew I had to do it. It wasn't fair to him. He'd been so good to me. And to Marley.

"We're not an item anymore," I said vaguely. "Nothing bad happened. I just realized that my heart wasn't fully in the relationship and he deserves someone who's all in."

Bentley's gaze flickered to the private office and back to me. "And are you all in?"

"I think so. I don't know exactly. We haven't addressed it yet."

"If I were you, I'd get back there right now and have the conversation before word reaches him about Tatiana," Tanya suggested. "Or he might slip right back into emotional paralysis."

She made a good point. "I was giving myself a little space after breaking up with Granger," I said. "I didn't want to rush straight into Alec's arms."

"I would," Tanya urged. "Go now. Get it in writing."

"Get it in blood," Bentley added.

I squinted. "I'm not getting a contract drawn up to solidify a relationship. He came to me and said he was ready. I'll take him at his word." All the same, I decided now would be a good time for the follow-up conversation.

"You have fifteen minutes before his call," Tanya whispered.

I scooted out of the chair and hurried to the back of the room. Alec's door was open. I hoped his vampire hearing hadn't picked up any of our conversation.

"Do you have a few minutes?" I asked, framed in the doorway.

He smiled and flashed his fangs. "For you? A lifetime." He waved me in.

"This good mood is…weird," I said. "I'm not used to it." I sat in the chair in front of his desk. "I feel like we should talk."

"Yes, I've been waiting," he said. "I thought it best to let things settle a bit before diving into that conversation."

"You mean you wanted to see whether I'd break things off with Granger."

He braided his fingers together. "And have you?"

"You know I have."

"I knew nothing of the sort." He paused. "I hoped the rumors were true, of course."

"They are," I said. I ignored the butterflies in my stomach. Before I indulged the giddy, besotted girl inside me, I had to put on my sensible hat for a moment. "If we're going to go full steam ahead with this…with us, I have a few ground rules."

His mouth twitched. "Such as?"

"We're going to start couples counseling…as a couple." Duh.

12

Surprise passed over his chiseled features. "Counseling?"

"That's right, and it's a deal breaker," I said. "We have to agree on the choice of counselor because that's fair, but there's no getting out of it. If you want to date me, we're getting professional help."

"So you are telling me that dating you requires professional help?"

I gave him the death stare. "Hardy har. You know what I'm saying."

He slotted his fingers together and rested them behind his head. "And what will we discuss in this session, given that we have not even embarked on a relationship yet?"

"Your issues. My issues. How we can make sure they don't destroy our relationship before it gets off the ground."

"This is very forward-thinking of you."

"I think we have a shot at being truly happy together," I admitted. "Let's not screw it up."

"Indeed." He moved his hands to the desk. "Any other requirements?"

"Marley," I said. "She adores you, but until I know this is going to have a relatively smooth trajectory, I don't want you at the cottage too often."

"You're protecting her."

"Of course I'm protecting her," I said vehemently. "She's my child. I don't want to parade you in front of her like a new father figure and then have you disappear when you decide you can't handle us. She's lost too many people already. We both have."

"As have I," Alec replied. "You cannot be a vampire without suffering loss. It is, sadly, part of the package of immortality."

"She's eleven. You're ancient. It's not the same."

"Do you really think I'll decide to disappear?" he asked, studying me.

"I don't have a clue what to expect from you, Alec," I said. "It hasn't exactly been an easy road to get here."

"No, I suppose not." He averted his gaze. "I do apologize for that."

"Apology accepted." I couldn't believe this was really happening. "You don't object to my conditions?"

"I told you I was ready and I meant it. I don't want to spend eternity missing you."

My spirits soared. Alec Hale and I were going to be an actual couple. No more yearning. No more pretending. I wanted to throw myself across his desk right now, but I held firm.

"One more thing," I said.

His brow lifted as if to say 'yes'?

I pointed. "I am not having sex on your desk."

He leaned back in his chair, confused. "I haven't suggested it."

"I know, but I'm picturing it right now and I've decided it'll hurt my lower back. It's not happening."

Alec suppressed a smile. "If you insist."

"And no sex for a while, no matter how badly I want it." Sweet baby Elvis, I needed to stop talking.

The vampire splayed his hands. "I am at your mercy."

"Good. I'm glad that's settled. I'll let you know when our first counseling session is and we can decide whether we want a repeat visit." I turned to go and heard him clear his throat.

"Just out of curiosity, Miss Rose," he said, "what constitutes 'a while' in your book?"

I glanced over my shoulder. "I'll let you know when I figure it out."

CHAPTER THREE

"YOU DIDN'T TELL Alec that Tatiana is in town?" My cousin Linnea stood in the large kitchen of Palmetto House, wide-eyed with horror.

"I don't want to be the messenger on that one," I said. I leaned my elbows on the counter, careful not to smudge the part she just cleaned. "We had enough to discuss. I dropped the counseling bombshell. Pretty sure that was all he could handle from me."

"I think counseling is a fantastic idea," Linnea said. "I wish I'd tried it sooner with Wyatt. Not that I'm convinced it would've helped. I guess it would've helped me recognize him earlier for who he really is." She sighed and continued wiping down the rest of the countertop. "That would've saved me a whole lot of heartache."

"Wyatt doesn't want to be in a committed relationship," I said. "That's nothing to do with you and I don't think any amount of counseling would change that."

She eyed me curiously. "But you think it will change Alec?"

"Not change him, help him," I said. "Help his communication skills. Help him process emotions in a healthy way. I don't know why he is the way he is."

"Maybe you don't want to find out," Linnea said, as she removed a tray and a teapot from the cupboard. "I told my guests I'd bring them tea. As they're my only guests right now, I need to make an effort."

I skipped right over the tea. I was still stuck on her previous statement. "What do you mean about not wanting to find out?"

"I mean, what if he's this way for horrible reasons that you're better off not knowing?" she replied. "He's a vampire. Maybe he's…done things he's not proud of. Things that make him want to avoid those he cares about."

My heart began to pound at the thought. "He's not a monster."

"Not now, but who knows what he was like before any of us knew him?" She added water and teabags to the pot and pulled her wand from the utensil drawer. She aimed her wand and said, "*Adducam ad ulcus.*"

"If counseling goes well, I guess I'll find out," I said.

"What has Mother said about the whole thing?" Linnea asked. "I'm sure she's pleased to be rid of another Nash." Aunt Hyacinth intensely disliked Wyatt and wasn't too keen on werewolves in general.

"I haven't told her," I said. "I've been holed up in the cottage trying to sleep away my guilt."

"You'd better tell her before Marley's party," Linnea said. "You don't want news like that spreading when Mother's hosting. She'll want the air cleared in advance."

"She probably knows," I said. "It's not like anyone in Starry Hollow has a working filter."

"Does Florian know?"

"Yes." He'd come to see me the very next day to get the

juicy details of my night with Granger. The conversation was not the one he anticipated.

"Then Mother knows. Florian has a huge mouth, especially when it comes to telling Mother things. It's how he keeps himself swaddled in boats and cars." She added two cups and a tiny pitcher of milk to the tray. "Would you like tea? I didn't even think to offer. Some hostess I am."

"I'm good, thanks. I have to get back to the cottage for my lesson with Marigold. Don't want to keep the magical drill sergeant waiting."

"Certainly not," Linnea said. "What time is Marley's orientation tomorrow?"

"First thing in the morning," I said. "I'm sure she'll be up half the night, which means I'll be up half the night."

Linnea stifled a laugh. "Worrying must run in the family."

"Not the whole family," I said. "I can't picture Florian worrying about much of anything."

Linnea pulled a face. "Great Goddess. What's that like? I feel like all I do is worry. About Bryn and Hudson. About the inn."

"Why would you worry about the inn?"

"Business is a little slow and I don't know if it's a downturn or a seasonal correction or what." She shrugged. "I need to advertise more. I'm just not very good at it."

"Can you hire someone? There must be agencies in town."

"Florian suggested that, too. There is one place Rick mentioned. I'll give them a call and see how expensive it might be."

"You don't think your mother would front you the money to pay for it?" I asked.

Linnea put a hand on her hip. "Do I look like her favorite child to you?"

It was no secret that Aunt Hyacinth favored her only son. It was hardly a coincidence that Florian was so feckless.

"If Florian doesn't get his act together, one of these days he will disappoint her in a way that's hard to come back from," I said.

"He seems to be doing all right with his work for the tourism board," Linnea said. "Aster certainly loves bossing him around, that's for sure."

"Consistency is the key," I said. "Florian can doing anything for a few months, until he tires of it."

"Like Delphine?" Linnea said. She picked up the tray, ready to deliver the tea to her guests.

"I appreciate that he made the effort with Delphine," I said. The librarian witch had been hopelessly in love with Florian for ages, but she wisely recognized that he wasn't ready to settle down and let him go.

"Poor Mother. She was very excited about Delphine," Linnea said. "She wants those Silver Moon babies that I failed to give her." Bryn and Hudson's werewolf gene dominated, so they didn't inherit Linnea's magic, much to Aunt Hyacinth's dismay.

"Your mother likes Rick," I said. "That's a pretty big deal." Although Linnea's minotaur boyfriend wasn't a wizard, he was a step up from a werewolf as far as Aunt Hyacinth was concerned.

Linnea smiled as she carried the tray toward the open doorway. "She does. And now that she has a merman suitor, she can hardly give me a hard time about a minotaur."

I laughed at the memory of Aunt Hyacinth being rescued from the rough waves of the ocean by a muscular merman. That was a sight I wouldn't soon forget. "How's that going?"

"I don't know," Linnea admitted. "She's been tightlipped about it."

"Then we'll pry those lips open at our next family dinner," I said.

Linnea's brow creased. "With magic?"

I blew a raspberry. "No, silly. The old-fashioned way. With alcohol."

"You're distracted," Marigold said in an accusatory tone. We sat across from each other at the dining table in Rose Cottage.

"We haven't even started yet," I objected. She'd only set out the Jenga box a second ago. The lid was still on.

"Still, I get the distinct sense that your mind is elsewhere. It's difficult to master psychic skills if your brain isn't fully engaged."

I stared at her. "Is this a mood thing? Haven't they sorted out your hormonal fluctuations yet?" Marigold recently began menopause and her hot flashes and mood swings had become a regular feature of our lessons.

"This is not about me, Ember. This is about you." She popped the lid off the box and scattered the contents on the table. "Anything you'd care to discuss before we begin?"

I crossed my arms. "I see what this is. You heard a rumor and you're looking for confirmation."

Marigold blinked innocently. "I have no idea what you're talking about. What rumor?"

"Nice try." I swiped a group of Jenga pieces and pulled them toward me. "I take it we're going to play a game of Jenga?"

Marigold yanked out the chair and sat. "One does not simply play a game of Jenga."

"Okay then. What does one simply do?"

"I am the Mistress-of-Psychic Skills," she said. "What do you think we're going to do?"

I looked from Marigold to the game pieces. "We're going to play using our psychic skills?"

She beamed. "Exactly. There will be touching of the pieces. You play using your telekinetic skills."

"What do I win if I beat you?" I asked.

"A sense of accomplishment," Marigold said with an air of sweeping confidence.

"Meh."

She balked. "Meh? That's how you describe a sense of accomplishment?"

"I have a sense of accomplishment when I remember to brush my teeth before bed. The stakes need to be higher here."

She drummed her fingers on the table. "I see. How about, if you win, I cook a romantic dinner for you and your significant other?"

I laughed. Loudly. "You're not subtle, are you?"

She shrugged. "It's never been my strong suit."

I tapped a Jenga piece on the table. "You really want to know what's going on, don't you?"

She leaned forward expectantly. "I do."

"Tell you what. If you win, I'll give you the inside scoop. If I win, you make dinner for Marley and me. She is my significant other, after all." I flashed a triumphant smile.

Marigold scowled before acquiescing. "Deal."

We built the tower and Marigold only smacked my hand away once when she wasn't pleased with the alignment.

"Do I go first?" I asked.

"I'll go in order to demonstrate," she said.

"You just want to show off your Carrie skills," I told her.

"Who's Carrie?" Marigold asked.

"Oh, she's right up your alley," I said. "I should introduce you one of these days." Stephen King's version of telekinesis would probably render Marigold mute for days. I mentally moved a viewing of *Carrie* to the top of my list.

Marigold sat quietly with her gaze pinned on a Jenga

piece. The wooden block slid out from its place, leaving the rest of the tower intact. "Your move," she said.

"You made it look far too easy," I said. It was one thing to move the piece. It was quite another to maneuver it without knocking over the tower.

"Practice makes perfect." She clapped cheerfully. "Come on, Ember. You can do it!"

And there was her cheerleader side. I'd been waiting for a glimpse of it today. Marigold never failed to cover both drill sergeant and cheerleader bases during our lessons.

I concentrated on the piece I wanted to move and focused my will. I pulled the wooden block toward me with my wand. At first it didn't seem like it was going to budge, but then it suddenly jerked out of the pile and flew across the room, skimming the floor until it smashed into the wall. It clattered on the floor and PP3 leaped off the sofa to investigate the intruder.

"Hey, the tower is still standing!" I proclaimed.

Marigold shook her head. "A true miracle." My phone buzzed in my pocket and Marigold shot me a reproachful look. "No phones during lessons, Ember. You know the rules."

"Marley is at school. I need to check if it's an emergency." I pulled out the phone and glanced at the screen. Tanya's face smiled back at me. She didn't call unless it was important. "Hi, Tanya."

"Ember, are you available?"

"I'm in a lesson with a psychic menace. Is everything okay?"

"You need to come quickly," the fairy said. "There's a problem."

"At your house?"

"Yes, please hurry and don't tell anyone."

I glanced at Marigold. "No one?"

"Not yet. Please hurry." She burst into tears before she hung up.

"I need to go," I said.

"But the game," Marigold objected.

"I'll explain later." Maybe. Right now I had to get to Tanya's house. The fairy never sounded distressed so something was definitely wrong.

I dashed from the cottage and hightailed it to my car. I put the pedal to the metal and blared Bruce Springsteen as I sped toward Tanya's house to calm my frazzled nerves. Whatever had happened, it was bad.

I was cruising down Coastline Drive when lights flashed in the rearview mirror. "You've got to be kidding me." I pulled over and slunk down in the seat. *Please don't be Granger. Please don't be…*Crap-on-a-stick. It was worse.

I rolled down my window. "Good afternoon, Deputy Bolan."

The leprechaun's scowl quickly morphed into a cruel smile. "This must be my lucky day, Rose. Do you know how fast you were driving?"

"Speed of light," I said.

"No, but you may as well have been," he replied. "Once you're ten miles over the speed limit, it doesn't much matter."

"It's an emergency," I told him, injecting the necessary sense of urgency into my voice.

He rested his chin on the open window. "Is that so? On a mission to break another man's heart?"

I sucked in a breath and tried to bite my tongue. "I would think you'd be thrilled with that particular outcome."

"Oh, I may have danced a little jig with my husband when I heard the news."

"Figures."

"That I'd dance? Hell's bells, yes."

"No, that you'd dance a jig. You probably don't know any other moves."

He scowled again. "Speeding tickets aren't cheap, you know."

"Just hurry up and write it then. I need to get to Tanya's. Something's happened."

Deputy Bolan peered at me. "There's really an emergency?"

"Yes!"

"What are you waiting for then?" he said, slapping the door. "Start your engine. I'll follow you."

The leprechaun scurried back to his car and kept the lights flashing. I pulled out in front of him and continued my race to Tanya's house. It suddenly occurred to me that Tanya's emergency had something to do with Alec. My fingers tightened on the wheel as I drove. I finally pulled to a stop in the driveway and hopped out. Deputy Bolan was behind me in a flash.

"What kind of driving was that?" he yelled.

"We call that offensive driving in New Jersey," I said.

"I call it crazy," he shot back. "You almost killed that Gorgon on the side of the road. How could you miss all those snakes?" He gesticulated wildly around his tiny head to indicate a mass of snakes.

"I was nowhere near her," I argued. I hurried to the front step and rang the bell. There was no answer. I rang it again.

The deputy gave me a solemn look. "Let's check the back."

I nodded. My pulse was throbbing. I hoped Tanya was okay. I hoped *Alec* was okay.

"Any chance you have your wand?" Deputy Bolan asked quietly.

"You think you need backup?" I asked, as we crept around the side of the house. I unlatched the gate and we rounded the corner. Tanya quickly came into view. She paced the length of the pool, her wings moving rapidly. She stopped when she saw me.

"Oh, Ember. Thank the gods." She didn't seem to register the deputy's presence. I wondered whether she could see him over the bushes.

"What's the matter?" I asked. "You sounded really upset." As I drew closer, the problem became glaringly obvious. Something had happened. Something terrible.

A body floated facedown in the pool. A set of crushed wings spread across her back and her long hair swirled around her, forming a hauntingly beautiful design. My hand flew to cover my mouth.

Deputy Bolan walked to the edge of the water and peered into the water. "Is that…?" He couldn't bring himself to finish the question.

"Yes," Tanya croaked. "It's my niece. It's Tatiana."

CHAPTER FOUR

TANYA BEGAN TO CRY. "I came home to drop off ingredients for a recipe Tatiana wanted to try later and found her like this."

Deputy Bolan fixed his attention on the older fairy. "Why did you call Miss Rose instead of the sheriff's office?"

"You know why," Tanya said without flinching.

The leprechaun rubbed his hands over his greenish face. "You can't be serious. You think Sheriff Nash is capable of something like this?"

"I have no idea," Tanya said. "But I know that he's nursing a deep wound right now and a traumatic blast from his past just blew into town. Tatiana isn't easy on others. She wouldn't have been gentle with him no matter what state he was in."

"Is that also why you called me instead of Alec?" I asked. Alec was the more logical choice to call in a crisis.

Tanya barely nodded. "I didn't want Bentley to know either. He's too loyal to Alec. Doesn't miss an opportunity to brown nose him either."

"You think I'm *not* loyal to Alec?" I asked.

She met my gaze. "I know you would do what's best for him." She looked at the deputy. "For both of them."

The leprechaun stared at the body in the water. "How's your magic, Rose? Can you help me get her out?"

I pulled out my wand and held it over the water. I had no idea what kind of spell to use to remove a dead body from a swimming pool.

Deputy Bolan nudged my arm. "Come on, Rose. What are you waiting for? Inspiration?"

"Pardon me. They don't exactly teach me this kind of thing in magic lessons." I focused my will the way I'd been taught and imagined the body rising. "*Consurgo*." Tatiana lifted about a half foot out of the water and then dropped back in with a huge splash that soaked us both. The leprechaun turned slowly to glower at me.

"Maybe put a little more muscle into it," he suggested tersely.

"Hey! I don't see you diving in there and dragging her out."

Out of nowhere, a black object zipped past us and used her teeth to grab Tatiana's dress by the back of the neck. The winged cat pulled the body out of the water and laid her to rest on the concrete. Tanya fluttered over and kneeled by her side.

"Bonkers?" I looked at my daughter's familiar. "What are you doing here?" I didn't know why I bothered to ask because I wouldn't understand the answer. I didn't have a psychic connection with the winged cat, only Marley did.

"Meow," Bonkers replied and flew off.

Deputy Bolan rolled the fairy onto her back. Her skin was blue and her eyes and mouth were open. Not an attractive look. Tanya turned away.

"She's definitely dead," the leprechaun said.

"Really, Captain Obvious? Are you sure you don't want to hedge your bets and go for a prognosis of mostly dead?"

He contemplated the body, ignoring my remark. "I won't call the sheriff. I think you were right to keep him out of this, Tanya. You and I can handle this, Rose. We've done it plenty of times before."

"Without Sheriff Nash?" I queried.

"That's an idea you need to get used to anyway," the deputy said.

While he continued to examine the body, I placed a comforting arm around Tanya. "I'm so sorry," I said. "I know how much you cared about her."

Tanya wiped the tears from her cheeks. "She was never easy, but she was family. I guess I can't say it's a shock that someone would want to hurt her."

"You don't think this was an accident?" I said. "Maybe she fell in and drowned?"

Tanya sniffed and fished a tissue from her pocket. "Tatiana was a strong swimmer. She spent the warmer days in her youth either here or at the beach."

"How do fairies swim?" I asked. "Don't your wings drag you down?"

"If we don't remove them or spell them first, they can make it complicated," she replied. "I don't often use the pool. It's mostly for guests. It was here when I bought the house years ago and I didn't feel right about filling it in."

Deputy Bolan stood and dusted off his knees. "We'll need to close this area off as a crime scene until we remove the body and gather all the evidence."

Tanya sucked in a shaky breath. "Not a problem. I'll get out of your hair." She moved forward to smooth back Tatiana's wet hair, but Deputy Bolan cleared his throat in protest.

"I'm sorry, Tanya, but I can't let you touch her," he said.

Tanya's eyes grew round. "Am I a suspect?"

"That's not what I'm implying," the deputy said. "I can't let you touch her because we risk disturbing the evidence."

"You moved her out of the pool!" Tanya said, her voice rising sharply. "I'd say that might disturb some evidence."

"I had to make sure she was dead," he explained. "If there was a chance to resuscitate her, I needed to know."

I squeezed Tanya's shoulder. "It'll be okay. Why don't you go inside until we're done here?"

The fairy's wings flapped, forcing her into the air. "That's probably for the best. I can't bear to see her like this anyway." She flew in through the back patio door and closed it behind her.

Deputy Bolan looked at me. "You sure about her?"

"She has no motive," I said. "In fact, she's probably the only one who would welcome Tatiana back to town. That's why she came to stay here."

"Except for whoever named Tatiana as a beneficiary," he replied. "Apparently, that paranormal didn't have a problem with her."

"If this is murder, then Tanya will be able to help us with the suspect list," I said. "She kept updated on all her niece's mischief. I think she felt a sense of responsibility just because they were related."

"You can't choose your relatives," Deputy Bolan said. "The gods know I'd trade my cousin Brent in a heartbeat."

"Trade him for what?" I asked.

The leprechaun shrugged. "A pack of gum. A deck of cards. Anything really."

I laughed. "That bad, huh?"

"The worst. He threw up at our wedding and claimed it was because the sight of us made him sick."

"Wow. He's that awful yet you still invited him?"

"Like I said, he's family." The deputy bent down to

examine Tatiana more closely. "I hate to break the news to the sheriff. He's had a helluva time recently."

My stomach knotted. Poor Granger.

"Are you sure this wasn't an accident?" I asked.

"No, we're looking at murder," he said. He lifted Tatiana's head and pointed. "Blunt force trauma to the back of the head, yet she was found facedown in the pool."

"I see what you mean."

"Somebody either whacked her on the back of the head and carried her to the pool unconscious or knocked her in the back of the head while she was standing close to the edge and she fell in. Either way, she drowned." Deputy Bolan scanned the pool area. "See anything here that could've been used as a weapon?"

I surveyed the concrete area around the pool but saw nothing obvious. "I'll check the other side of the fence." I searched the entire backyard but came up empty-handed. It was only when I headed back to the deputy that I noticed it.

A broken chair leg.

It was only slightly bent so that the chair was still upright but I could tell it was tilted. "Could someone have hit her with the chair?" I pointed at the furniture.

Deputy Bolan went over to inspect the chair leg. "I'll have the examiner confirm, but I bet the condition of the chair is consistent with her head injury. I should seal off the area now. Let the sheriff know, too."

I glanced uneasily at Deputy Bolan. "If you're going to call him, I should probably get out of earshot." If the deputy mentioned my name, I didn't want to accidentally overhear the sheriff's response.

"Good thinking," the leprechaun replied. "Before you go, here." He took a slip of paper from his pocket and handed it to me.

I glanced down at it. "What's this?"

"Your speeding ticket. You didn't think I'd let you off the hook, did you?"

I shook the paper at him. "What do you think the sheriff will say when he finds out? He'll assume you targeted me. Is that what you want? To get on your boss's bad side after a horrible breakup? After this." I waved my arm in Tatiana's direction.

The deputy pressed his tiny lips together. Finally, he reached out and snatched the ticket. "Fine, but you're on my list, Rose."

"The only list we should be concerned with right now is the one with Tatiana's murder suspects," I said. "I'll go and talk to Tanya on my way out."

The deputy hesitated. "You'll help me with this case, won't you, Rose? We're going to have to treat the sheriff as a suspect. Avoid any appearance of impropriety."

"And you think *I'm* the best person for the job? I appear improper all the time. It's practically my job."

"This is Tatiana," the deputy said. "She left destruction in her wake whenever she went to the grocery store. I can do this without help, but it'll take a lot longer and that means extended misery for Sheriff Nash." He gave me a pointed look. "Don't you think the poor guy has suffered enough?"

"Fine," I said, relenting. "I'll help."

"Great," Deputy Bolan said. "I'll expect you at the office tomorrow afternoon. Bring coffee. Lots of cream."

I folded my arms. "You're kidding, right?"

"Not at all," the deputy replied. "The coffee at the sheriff's office is terrible."

I groaned and stomped off toward the house to talk to Tanya. This day had turned out to be a terrible time to decide to rejoin the land of the living.

. . .

I flipped through a recipe book trying to prepare a healthy dinner for Marley. I ended up staying later with Tanya than I anticipated because she was too upset to leave by herself. Marley was relaxing in her bedroom after spending time after school with friends in honor of her last day at the middle school. I hoped to prepare a special meal to celebrate and, by special, I meant not burned, mutilated, or inedible.

I rushed around the kitchen, gathering ingredients or substitutes for ingredients I didn't have, which was most items. I was about to break an egg on the side of a bowl when PP3's bark jolted me. I missed the bowl completely and smashed the egg into the counter.

Fantastic.

I rinsed off my hands and hurried to the door to see what set off the dog. Before I reached the door, it flew open and Raoul staggered into the cottage. He looked filthy—even filthier than usual for a dumpster diving trash panda.

"Raoul, what happened to you?" Marley asked, hurrying down the steps.

I examined the raccoon's messy fur and spotted a few pieces of trash stuck to his fur. "You look like you went swimming in Garbage Lake."

His expression grew wistful. *There's a Garbage Lake?*

I groaned in disgust. "No, it's just an expression. Why do you look like you lost a toaster in a brawl at the dump?"

Because I did, Raoul said glumly. *Except it was a crockpot, not a toaster. There's a new guy hanging around the dump and he's decided I'm the one he wants to keep out. Some of the pea-brained animals have chosen to gang up with him.*

I stared at him. "Wait. You're being bullied at the dump?"

He tapped his claws together. *I tried to fight him today. It didn't go well.*

"What kind of animal is he?" I asked.

Raoul's gaze dropped to the floor. *A big one. Huge.*

31

"A bear?" I asked.

Not that big, but more vicious. He's like an Orc with wings.

"Did you just make a *Lord of the Rings* reference?" I asked.

What? I love Gandalf, Raoul said. *He's my spirit animal.*

"Technically, you're *my* spirit animal," I said.

No, I'm your familiar, he said. *It's different.*

"So what's the animal? A junkyard dog?"

He mumbled something unintelligible.

I strained to listen. "Did you say a coyote?"

A crow.

I thought I'd misheard him. "Did you just say a crow? As in the bird?"

He nodded. *This one is a nasty piece of work. Wears a red rubber band around his leg. Thinks it makes him look tough, but it just makes him look like he fell into the pile of discarded school supplies.*

I laughed. "Raoul, you have to be bigger than this guy."

He has wings. Raoul flapped his front legs. *He uses them to stay out of reach and then swoops down to attack.*

"Not even a raven, huh? Just an ordinary crow?"

Raoul huffed. *Don't make me feel worse about it. I've completely lost my street cred.*

"What about Bonkers?" I suggested. "She has wings. She could give the crow a hard time from the air."

"Bonkers would be happy to help," Marley interjected. "I'll call to her now."

Raoul scoffed. *Bonkers is adorable. The crow won't be worried about a flying cat.*

"Crows are afraid of cats, aren't they?" I asked.

Not ones that you want to snuggle with, Raoul objected.

"Bonkers is tougher than she looks," Marley said. "She won't let you down." The gray and white winged cat appeared in the window and Marley opened the door to let her in. The flying kitten swooped through the room and perched on the top of the sofa. My heart melted a little. Darn. Raoul wasn't wrong. Bonkers was adorable. Maybe we did need a fiercer opponent.

What's the plan? Raoul asked. *Have Bonkers escort me to the dump like she's my bodyguard? Purr and meow in his direction?*

"You have to stand up to a bully or they'll just keep pushing," I said.

Sounds like you have experience, Raoul said. *How many people had to stand up to you before you stopped?*

"Hey!" I swatted at him with a dishtowel. "I was never a bully."

You're from New Jersey, Raoul said. *I thought it was part of the package. I've seen The Sopranos.*

"How do you have all this time to watch television?" I asked.

It's lessened considerably since I met you, Raoul said.

"All right, let me know the next time you decide to go to the dump and we'll send you with Bonkers," I said. I had enough on my plate right now. I didn't need to add 'throwdown at the trash heap' to my list.

"I've told Bonkers the story," Marley said. "She's totally on board. She said crows are known as dumpster dive bombers in the trash world."

There's a trash world? Raoul asked wistfully.

"Only in your dreams," I replied.

The raccoon sniffed the air. *Do I smell food?*

I heaved a sigh, remembering my dinner attempt. "You smell a cracked egg."

That counts as food, he said.

"I'm making a special dinner for Marley," I said. Or trying.

What is it?

"Pancakes," I blurted. Because, at this point, that was the only meal I'd be capable of.

33

Isn't that a breakfast dish? Raoul asked.

"Are you criticizing my food offering?" I asked. "Because you don't need to eat it."

"Yay, pancakes!" Marley jumped and down, clapping. "One of my favorites. Can we add chocolate chips and whipped cream?"

"Why don't we save ourselves the trouble and just stuff them full of straight sugar?" I suggested with a touch of sarcasm.

Raoul rubbed his stomach. *Perfect.*

We assembled in the kitchen so that I could make the pancakes. Marley begged to help, so we finished much more quickly. I filled them in on Tatiana while we ate.

"I feel horrible for Tanya and Sheriff Nash," Marley said.

"What about Alec?" I asked. He'd been involved with Tatiana, too, once upon a time.

"Alec not only loves you, but you left the sheriff to be with him," Marley said. "This won't hit Alec nearly as hard. Not to mention the sheriff will have to investigate his ex-girlfriend's murder. That'll be rough."

"He has to be cleared first," I said.

Marley choked on her chocolate milk. "He's a suspect?"

I nodded. "So is Alec for now. Anyone in town with an axe to grind."

Marley swallowed another forkful of pancake. "I'd rule them out first so you don't have that hanging over your heads and then Sheriff Nash can take back control of the investigation."

"What's the rush?" I asked. "You don't think your mother can handle it? As it happens, I'm meeting him at the sheriff's office tomorrow afternoon, after your orientation at the academy. We're going to work our way through the suspect list together. *Vox Populi* will want to cover the murder, too, so it's a win-win."

It's nice when murder can be considered a win-win, Raoul said.

I pointed my fork at him and glared. "The sooner we crack this case, the better for everyone in town."

She suppressed a laugh. "You and Deputy Bolan working together? Without causing each other bodily harm?"

I polished off the last of my pancake. "The little green man and I are willing to set aside our differences for the sake of the sheriff. He deserves our complete cooperation." I felt very grown up making such a mature statement.

Whether I could stick to it or not was a different story.

CHAPTER FIVE

The Black Cloak Academy reminded me of those movies where wealthy, privileged kids in crested blazers congregated to haze each other and inflict other horrible tortures on those less fortunate.

And now Marley would be one of them.

Granted, in lieu of blazers they wore black cloaks, but the cloaks were stitched with a house crest and pointy hats were part of the uniform albeit for outdoor use only. Marley was relieved because she disliked the way she looked in hats. Something about the shape of her head.

"Mom, can you get over this place?" Marley asked, nearly breathless.

It was hard to believe the academy was smack in the middle of Starry Hollow. The academy grounds were idyllic. A small lake, majestic trees, sweeping acreage, stables—there was even a picturesque bridge over a babbling brook. Marley marveled at her new surroundings.

"This is as wonderful as Thornhold," she said.

"With the bonus of no Aunt Hyacinth," I added.

She smiled. "I'm sure there will be teachers even worse than she is."

I slung an arm along her shoulders and squeezed. "For your sake, you'd better hope not."

Marley tipped her head back and laughed and my heart swelled. Holy Happy Child. I felt so grateful right now. I hoped the inside was every bit as awesome as the outside.

"So many witches and wizards in our family went to school here and now I get to be one of them." She sighed and I felt her vibrations of contentment.

We strode through the open gates and arrived at an impressive set of oak doors. Marley didn't hesitate. She tugged on the golden rope that dangled alongside the door. Although we didn't hear the sound of a chime or bell, the door creaked open and a single eye peeked out at us. Not because that was the only one we could see, but because it was the only one he had.

"Cyclops," Marley whispered, enthralled.

The door opened fully and a man the size of Frankenstein with a single eye blinked down at us. "You must be here for orientation. I'm Bud. Good to meet you."

Bud? That seemed an unlikely name for a cyclops, but what did I know about them? "And what do you do here, Bud?" I asked.

"I'm the academy manager," Bud replied. "I take care of the grounds and the animals."

"Animals," Marley repeated.

"Oh, you like animals, do you?" Bud smiled at her, revealing a set of startlingly straight and white teeth. I'd expected stained and crooked chompers, not a commercial for Crest Whitestrips.

"I do," Marley replied.

"Well, I'll be meeting you later for a tour of the outside," Bud said. He patted her on the head. "Looking forward to it."

"Me, too," Marley said.

"Go on in," Bud said. "There are a few others already in there waiting. Orientation is always a lot of fun."

The corridor was dim and narrow with high ceilings and a floor made of gray slate. Portraits of past teachers cluttered the wall, esteemed witches and wizards no doubt. I didn't recognize most of the names.

"Mom, look! She's holding my wand." Marley ran to one of the portraits and pointed. Sure enough, a witch posed with a wand in her hand that looked remarkably similar to the one Marley received from Aunt Hyacinth for her eleventh birthday. With its well-worn groove marks and runes along the ancient handle, it was unmistakable.

"The plaque says her name is Ivy," I said. "We'll have to ask about her."

"She looks like you with light hair," Marley said.

"Do you think?" I studied the witch's features. The witch in the portrait sported the white-blond hair associated with the Rose family.

"The shape of her eyes and her mouth," Marley said.

"Then she must look like you, too," I said, ruffling her hair. Marley was a mini-me. Everybody said so.

Marley stared at the portrait in awe. "I can't wait to know more. I just know my wand has a history. I can feel it." I didn't doubt it. I remembered the emotions that had flooded me when I'd held the wand during a previous psychic skills lesson with Marigold. Strength, power, disappointment, grief, love...I'd felt them all at once and the experience had been overwhelming. And now here she was framed on the academy wall. Even from beyond the grave, Ivy had a story to tell and I was determined to uncover it.

We continued down the corridor and located the assembly room where a small group was already gathered. Five new recruits and their parents. I balked when I realized that I was the only single parent among them. It wasn't so unusual, was it? A tall witch in a red cloak stepped forward. Her brilliant white hair was pulled back in a tight bun that accentuated her sharp features.

"Welcome to orientation. You must be Marley," the witch said. "I'm Poppy Lux-Harp, the headmistress of this fine institution."

Poppy looked vaguely familiar. I'd probably seen her at council meetings and not been introduced. Knowing me, we probably *had* been introduced and I'd forgotten.

"Nice to meet you," Marley said. "I'm very excited to be here."

"I can tell," Poppy said. "Your energy is filling in the room." Marley beamed in response. "And you must be her mother. I've seen you at the monthly meetings, but we haven't been properly introduced."

I extended my hand. "Ember Rose."

Poppy's slender hand squeezed mine. "I look forward to having another Rose under this roof. Always a pleasure."

"Even Florian?"

Poppy suppressed a smile. "Florian Rose-Muldoon was a delightful wizard. Full of mischief."

"Full of something," I mumbled.

Poppy introduced us to the other new pupils and their parents. One was new in town. Two came from a private school for witches and wizards that hadn't come into their magic yet. Another had been homeschooled. Only one was from the public school like Marley, a wizard called Coriander. They recognized each other, but that was the extent of their familiarity.

Poppy gave us a guided tour of the building, showing each classroom. We were quiet for the lessons in session and I watched Marley's eyes widen as she absorbed her surroundings. We saw floating candles and glowing magic orbs and a greenhouse that dwarfed the one at the public school.

Coriander's mother sidled up to me. "I'm a huge fan of your aunt. I attend council meetings just to listen to her speak."

"Her kaftans alone are worth the price of admission," I joked.

"She oozes elegance and confidence." The witch inhaled sharply. "Is she the same way at home or is it just a performance?"

"Oh, it's her natural state," I assured the witch. "Makes for interesting Sunday dinners."

She laughed. "I can imagine. I'm Juniper, by the way."

"Nice to meet you," I said. Juniper seemed nice and, dare I say, normal. I hadn't had the best luck with school mothers, although I still liked the idea of them. As Florian kept insisting, a mom friend would be good for me. I had Linnea and Aster, of course, but they were family. Maybe the academy would be different for me as well as for Marley. One could hope.

"Has Marley been freaking out about her magic as much as my son?" Juniper asked. Her auburn curls were a far cry from her son's pale blond mop.

"It was a nailbiter," I admitted. "Her father's pure human, so it was touch and go there until the very end."

Juniper gave me a curious look. "All human? Well, I suppose the blood of the One True Witch runs strong enough for both of you."

I didn't want to focus on our ancestry. I thought the whole fixation on the One True Witch was unnecessary, but I knew Starry Hollow loved their pecking order as much as a hen house. Between the Rose name and the One True Witch distinction, Marley and I were destined to be put on an undeserved pedestal.

"Are you and your husband both members of the coven?" I queried.

"Oh, yes," Juniper replied. "Our parents were very keen for us to marry one of our own. Luckily for us, we met each other and decided it was a good idea."

No wonder she was a fan of Aunt Hyacinth's. She sang the same tune. As much as my aunt liked Alec, I knew she'd still prefer that I settle down with a nice wizard and produce more magical heirs. She was a mixed bag, my aunt. A feminist on the one hand, but old-fashioned in her thinking on the other.

We poked our heads in a variety of classrooms. Most were in session, so we only received a brief introduction before moving on to the next room. Everyone seemed friendly so far.

"Ah, what luck. Here is one of our new teachers without a room full of pupils," Poppy said.

We stopped in the doorway of an empty classroom, except for a man on his knees in the middle of the floor. He appeared to be using an academy shirt to wipe up orange liquid. He craned his neck to see us.

"Hello there. Just cleaning up a small spill," he said. "Nothing to be concerned about. It's only toxic when it touches bare skin." It was only then that I noticed his gloves.

"Perry Packard is teaching the Science of Magic," Poppy said. "He came highly recommended from a witchcraft school in Europe."

Perry gave us a thumbs up and went back to scrubbing.

"The Science of Magic sounds cool," Marley said.

"Science is boring," Coriander said. "Magic is cool."

"We lost our previous teacher unexpectedly," Poppy said, "so we feel fortunate to have Mr. Packard arrive on such short notice."

"Was that Mr. Sewell?" one of the parents asked.

"Yes, it was," Poppy said. "He performed with fireballs outside of academy hours, a beloved hobby, and there was an unfortunate incident with a strong easterly wind."

Yikes. "Is he okay?" I asked.

Poppy offered a sympathetic smile. "He will be...in time."

"He has a large family, doesn't he?" Juniper asked. "I seem to recall seeing the Sewell brood in town."

"Five children," Poppy said. "A very capable wife, though. I have no doubt they'll manage."

"Raising a family is hard," Juniper said.

Perry glanced up from the spill. "Not if they're buried close enough to each other."

Juniper blinked, as though she'd misheard the necromancer. "Pardon?

"What?" Realizing his faux pas, Perry blushed furiously and turned back to his task.

I coughed a laugh and quickly covered my mouth.

"Let's move on, shall we?" Poppy said.

Marley continued to linger in the doorway, so I stayed with her while the rest of the tour group carried on.

"Are you a vampire?" Marley asked.

Perry finished mopping up the spill and rose to his feet. "No, why?"

"Your comment made me think maybe you were," Marley said shyly.

Perry's blush returned. "Oh, you heard that, did you?" He chuckled awkwardly. "A slip of the tongue."

"But you know something about raising the dead," I said, and the realization hit me. "Are you a necromancer?"

Perry brought his finger to his lips and shushed me. "The academy does not want me to parade this information in front of the parents. They believe it will cause too much trouble."

"Why?" Marley asked.

"Necromancy is illegal here," Perry said. "They worry I will be getting their children into trouble."

"But you won't be teaching us necromancy," Marley said. "You're teaching the Science of Magic, and I can't wait for your class."

He smiled and the effect was endearing. "Thank you. What is your name, young witch?"

"Marley," she said. "I'm sort of new to Starry Hollow, like you."

"Wonderful. I hope, like me, you are beyond thrilled to be here," Perry said. "It is good to be away from my bickering family. The stress…It gets to be too much at times."

"Where are you from?" Marley asked.

"My family is originally from Eastern Europe, although too many have settled along the coast here." His sigh was tinged with regret. Suddenly, his smile broadened. "But none in Starry Hollow. I am free to be myself here." He motioned to the orange stain on the floor. "Which can be both good and bad."

"You weren't free to be yourself with your family?" Marley asked. She looked at me and I knew exactly what she was thinking. She and I were completely and totally ourselves with each other, for better or worse.

He wiped his brow and gave a nervous chuckle. "Well, it is complicated, as families often are." He pulled the cloth away, realizing he'd used the same cloth to wipe his brow that he'd used on the floor. "Do I have orange on my forehead?"

"No," I said.

"Phew. I was not joking about its toxicity."

"Are you really a necromancer?" Marley asked.

Perry's finger shot to his lips again. "It is to be our secret."

"It isn't appropriate to have secrets with your students," Marley said, "especially a young girl. It would give the wrong impression." She glanced at me for approval. "Right, Mom?"

I took her hand. "Normally, I'd agree with you, but under the circumstances, Mr. Packard is right to be wary. Necromancy is illegal and parents would likely be uneasy about allowing him to teach here."

"It is a role that has been handed down in my family for centuries," Perry explained. "I can no more escape it than you can escape the color of your eyes."

"I can wear colored contact lenses," Marley said. "Or glamour them to look brown."

"And I can disguise myself as a Science of Magic teacher," Perry said with a wink.

"We should probably catch up to the others," I said. "It was great to meet you."

"I eagerly await your presence in my class, Marley," the necromancer said with a slight bow.

Marley let out a small squeak. "Thanks, I'll see you tomorrow."

The rest of the tour was rudimentary. Bathrooms. Water fountains. Cafeteria. I could tell Marley was itching to move on to more interesting topics. Finally, we arrived back at the main entrance.

"We eagerly await your arrival tomorrow as new students of the Black Cloak Academy," Poppy said, as she waved us off.

Marley practically floated across the academy grounds as we headed home. "This is the best day ever. I'm going to love it here."

"Someone's not going to sleep tonight," I said.

Marley's cheeks turned pink. "Can I have a sleep potion? I don't want to be groggy my first day. What if I don't perform as well as the other students?" The anxiety was clear as a bell and my own worry crept in. Marley had been doing so well since our move here. What if the Black Cloak Academy pressed all her anxiety buttons?

She continued to clasp my hand and I enjoyed the slight pressure of it, the reminder that she was still my little girl. Still the child I bore and raised and loved beyond measure. Magic was her dream. This academy was her dream and it was my job to support her. And if the anxiety demons came to claim her, then we'd fight them together.

CHAPTER SIX

"DID YOU BRING THE COFFEE?" Deputy Bolan asked. I'd dropped Marley off at Florian's man cave after orientation so that I could arrive at the sheriff's office at the appointed time.

"That's your concern?" I asked. I handed him the coffee I bought from the Caffeinated Cauldron. Marley was right—I didn't want the investigation to end in bodily harm. It was my civic duty to co-exist with Deputy Bolan and solve the case without further bloodshed.

"Tanya came up with a solid list of suspects," the deputy said.

"No surprise there," I said. "She's pretty well-versed in Tatiana's checkered past."

"I thought we'd get the toughest one out of the way first," the leprechaun said.

My gut twisted. "Sheriff Nash?"

He nodded. "I haven't told him yet, but I think he knows it's coming."

"Well, he obviously knows he wasn't the first one called to the crime scene."

"There's a magic mirror in interrogation room two," the deputy said.

My brow lifted. "A magic mirror? Why?"

"So you can see what's happening during the interrogation without them seeing you."

I laughed. "That's not magic. That's just a standard 2-way mirror."

The leprechaun frowned. "There's a mirror that doesn't reflect your image. If that's not magic, then I don't know what is. Anyway, the point is if you stay on the other side of the mirror, you can take notes."

"No way," I said. "I need to be in there."

"You can't question him with me," Deputy Bolan said. "It'll be too distracting, plus you have no experience."

"No experience?" I repeated. "What do you think I do as a reporter? I ask tough questions."

The deputy slurped his coffee. "It's not the same."

"Well, you can't interrogate your boss by yourself," I replied. "You're too biased. Besides, you know each other too well. He could manipulate you if he really wanted to."

"And you're still feeling guilty about dumping him," he shot back. "I bet he could wrap you around his finger, too."

We stared at each other for a brief moment. "We need someone impartial, but someone who knows how to get answers," I finally said.

"But who?" He scratched his head. "Your aunt?"

"No way. She's biased against werewolves," I said. And Nash brothers in general. "What about a seer?"

"You want to ask a psychic to tell us who killed Tatiana?" He sounded incredulous.

"No, but a good seer knows how to ask the right probing questions. Am I right?"

Deputy Bolan leaned against the wall and folded his arms. "I'm listening."

"Veronica," I said simply.

He pondered the suggestion. Veronica had a place over on Seers' Row. Despite her shrill voice, she and her assistant, Jericho, were highly regarded in the psychic community. Plus, she predicted Deputy Bolan's wedding, so he had a soft spot for her.

"The other option is we take him to Casper's Revenge and let the ghosts sort him out," I said.

The leprechaun shuddered. "Not a fan of that place."

I didn't blame him. The haunted inn was notorious for a couple of its tough-talking apparitional inhabitants. "Okay then. Let's see if we can get Veronica over here. Tell her what we need."

"I'll call and explain the situation," he offered. "It needs to be official."

"We're asking a moody psychic to grill the sheriff on whether he murdered his ex-girlfriend," I said. "I think we lost 'official' a few miles back."

Deputy Bolan looked me in the eye. "He can't be guilty, can he?"

"The only way to rule him out for sure is to find the killer," I said.

"But we both know him well," the deputy pressed. "We know what he's capable of…and what he's not."

"I can't see Granger murdering anyone," I admitted. "Werewolf or not, he's the gentlest guy I know."

Deputy Bolan smirked. "Don't let your new boyfriend hear you say that."

I ignored the remark. "Still, we have to do this right so that no one in town thinks the sheriff's office is covering for him. They'll want to know that the investigation is above reproach."

"Maybe I should call in the sheriff from Dewdrop Hills," the leprechaun said. He quickly shook his head. "No, that won't work. He and Sheriff Nash don't like each other. Sheriff Sherman would welcome the chance to skewer him."

"Veronica it is then," I said. "I bet she's available now. She's not that busy during business hours."

Deputy Bolan arched a thin eyebrow. "Are you giving me orders, Rose?" He tapped the badge on his chest. "I'm pretty sure I'm the deputy around here."

I rolled my eyes. "Relax. You don't need to pee a circle around the room. I consider this a collaborative effort."

He sniffed. "I'm a leprechaun. We don't pee...around rooms."

I patted his shoulder. "Glad to hear it. I'll hang around until Veronica gets here. Even if I can't be in the room, I at least want to listen in via your magic mirror." I snorted.

"It is magic, Rose," he insisted.

Half an hour later I was squared away behind the double mirror while Veronica and Jericho set up shop in the interrogation room. I wasn't sure why she bothered to bring her crystal ball. Habit, most likely.

Sheriff Nash sauntered into the room. I was surprised by how nonchalant he seemed. Almost amused. Granted, he was entering his own interrogation room to be confronted with a crystal ball, but still. He settled into the chair and set his gaze on Veronica. "Ready when you are."

"I'm ready." Veronica rolled up her angel sleeves, which was more difficult than it sounds because the fabric was so wide at the end that it kept unrolling the moment she let go. She swatted in frustration at the material before turning her full attention to the sheriff. "Do you know why you're here?"

"Deputy Bolan and I had a brief discussion," he replied. "I'll play along for the sake of the investigation."

"Play along?" Deputy Bolan muttered beside me. "It's not a game, Sheriff."

"Did you kill your ex-girlfriend?" Veronica asked, staring at him intently.

The sheriff relaxed in his chair. "Which one?"

"Does it matter?" Jericho sputtered from behind the seer. "The answer should be an unequivocal no!"

The sheriff grinned. "Word of advice? Don't take this show on the road."

Veronica didn't respond. Instead, she gazed into her crystal ball. "I'm seeing a lot of emotions at play for you this week. Perhaps you were angry and bitter when you ran into her. Couldn't contain your volatile emotions."

"I saw Ember in the hallway on my way in here and I felt neither of those emotions," he replied.

I froze at the mention of my name. He'd seen me? Did he know I was in here now, watching?

"What did you feel then?" Veronica asked.

The werewolf hesitated, his gaze flicking to the mirror before returning to Veronica. Yep. He knew I was here.

"Nothing," he said. My chest squeezed. I hated knowing that I was responsible for the hurt in his dark eyes.

Veronica stood and slammed her hands against the crystal ball, causing the sheriff to jump. "And is that also what you felt after you murdered Tatiana? Nothing?"

Sheriff Nash waved his hands. "Whoa, whoa. I did not kill Tatiana."

Veronica apologized to the crystal ball and caressed it before sitting down again. "Prove it."

"I do believe it's innocent until proven guilty here, oh merciful one," Jericho said.

Veronica twisted in her seat to glare at her bubbly assistant. "Put a lid on it, Jericho!" She turned back to the sheriff. "Did you see Tatiana since her return to Starry Hollow?" She tapped her nails on the crystal ball. "And don't lie. I can see the truth right in here."

"Then I don't suppose you need me to answer," he replied smoothly.

"Answer me!" Veronica shrieked.

I cut a worried glance at Deputy Bolan. I was starting to regret bringing in the seer.

"She's unhinged," the leprechaun said.

"I'm pretty sure that's hinged for Veronica," I said.

The sheriff threaded his fingers together and rested them on his knee. "Yeah, I saw Tatiana."

What? A lump formed in my throat. When?

"When was that?" Veronica asked.

"The day after she cast her long shadow over this town," he said.

"He means the day after she arrived in Starry Hollow, most beauteous creature," Jericho said in a stage whisper.

"I understand similes, Jericho," she snapped.

The dwarf held up a chubby finger. "Actually, it's not a simile. It's a…"

"Silence!" she screeched. "And where did you see Tatiana?"

The sheriff was incredibly calm during this unorthodox procedure. I couldn't tell whether it was because he figured Veronica wouldn't get the truth out of him, or because he was telling the truth and felt comfortable that everything would shake out as it should. For the sake of my sanity, I had to believe it was the latter.

"It was an accident," the sheriff said.

"The murder?" Veronica pressed.

He rolled his eyes. "No, the meeting. She was on her way into the salon to get her nails done and I was patrolling the block."

"Since when does he patrol a block?" Deputy Bolan said under his breath.

"Just the block?" Veronica queried.

"At the time, yes," the sheriff said.

"Which salon?" Veronica asked.

"Glitter Me This," he replied.

"That's right near my office," I said. Even though he was a foot below me, I felt the deputy's pointed gaze. I knew what he was thinking because I had the same thought. He wasn't patrolling. He was...

"Why were you patrolling that block, Sheriff?" Jericho asked. "Has there been trouble there?"

Veronica jerked her head in the dwarf's direction. "I ask the questions here."

"Technically, I ask the questions here," the sheriff said. "Are we about finished? I have work to do."

"Answer Jericho's question," Veronica ordered.

The sheriff's jaw tightened. "I had a few things I wanted to check on," he said vaguely.

A few things like me.

"Have you noticed him lurking around *Vox Populi?*" Deputy Bolan asked.

I shook my head. I had no doubt he was careful not to be spotted. He would've been mortified to run into Alec. To my knowledge, they hadn't seen each other since I broke up with the sheriff.

"And what did you say to each other?" Veronica asked.

"I made polite inquiries, the way my family taught me," he replied.

"Did you tell her she looked good?" Veronica asked. "That you still remembered the way her hair felt when you slid your fingers through it?"

The sheriff narrowed his eyes. "I don't believe I did, no."

"Good, because that would've been inappropriate," Veronica said. "Did you ask why she was in town?"

"I did. She said she'd been left an inheritance and she'd come to claim it," he said. "That was easy enough to believe."

"Did she say who would be foolish enough to leave her anything of value?" Veronica asked.

Deputy Bolan smacked his forehead. "For a seer, she does not do subtle."

"No, and I wasn't interested in the details," the sheriff said.

"Did she tell you where she was staying in town?" Veronica asked.

"No, but I assumed she was with her aunt. Tanya's the only one I can think of who'd allow it." The sheriff's cheek pulsed with tension. "It was a quick and painless conversation. I had no reason to linger and no reason to kill her. My feelings for Tatiana are long over and, let's face it, they were never real anyway."

Veronica stood and banged on the mirror. "Anything else you want me to ask? I think I covered it." She pressed her forehead against the glass right in front of me.

"You could ask me where I was at the time of death," the sheriff said.

"Excellent notion, Sheriff," Jericho said, smiling affably.

Veronica returned to her seat. "And where were you at the time of death, whenever that was?"

Sheriff Nash stroked the stubble on his chin, as though he hadn't already thought through the answer. "Patrolling."

"Alone?" Veronica asked.

"I do a lot of that," he said. "In case you haven't noticed, it's a small town. Deputy Bolan and I manage just fine."

"Where were you patrolling this time?" Veronica asked. "Another block?"

A scowl passed over his rugged features. "A residential neighborhood."

Veronica leaned forward. "Which one? The one where Tatiana was staying?"

"No," he said simply. "Nowhere near."

"You said yourself it's a small town," Veronica told him. "It had to be somewhere near."

"She's better at this than I expected," Deputy Bolan said.

"Never underestimate the power of a woman with a headscarf and a shiny object," I replied.

"Near Castledown," the sheriff said quietly.

The deputy looked at me. "Isn't that the mansion closest to Thornhold?"

It was.

"Did anyone see you?" Veronica asked.

"Are you asking for an alibi?" the sheriff asked.

"Of course," Veronica replied. "That's SOP."

"Standard Operating Procedure," Jericho added.

A grin tugged at the corners of the sheriff's mouth. "Yes, I'm familiar with the term. As a matter of fact, I passed a couple of folks during that time. Florian Rose-Muldoon and Maya Briggs."

He'd seen Florian, so my cousin knew that the sheriff had been wandering nearby, not that I'd been home at the time.

"Maya Briggs lives at Castledown, doesn't she?" Veronica asked.

"That she does. She was out for a walk. Florian was..." The sheriff frowned. "Who the hell knows what Florian's ever doing? I saw him and we chatted for a few minutes. Feel free to check with them both."

I'd certainly be talking to Florian about this. Why didn't he tell me that I had a grieving stalker? Ugh. The knowledge only made me feel worse.

"Is that all your questions?" Veronica called over her shoulder.

Deputy Bolan knocked on the glass to indicate yes.

"You might want to let your puppet masters know that Dana Ellsworth would be my first stop for questioning," the sheriff said. "She and Tatiana were best friends back in the day. Inseparable."

Deputy Bolan nodded. "She's on Tanya's list."

"Thank you," Veronica said. "You're free to go, hon, but don't leave town. We might not be finished with you yet."

"No worries. I'm not going anywhere," Sheriff Nash said. "No matter how tough things get, I'm not the type to cut and run."

"Ooh, burn," the deputy said. I caught the gleeful look in his beady eye.

Outwardly, I remained unruffled. "Try not to get so much joy out of a crappy situation, at least in my presence."

The leprechaun's delight faded. "You're right, Rose. I'm sorry. To be honest, I actually hate seeing him like this. I hope it passes soon. I miss the old sheriff."

I watched as the sheriff stood, his expression inscrutable. His hair was rumpled and there were dark circles under his eyes. He left the interrogation room without another word. "Finally," I said, releasing a breath, "something we can agree on."

CHAPTER SEVEN

I PAGED through Marley's ancient grimoire, given to her by Aunt Hyacinth. I treated each page with care because the poor book looked like it had been buried underground for decades, before being dug up, washed, and placed in a deep fryer.

"I like that they had the foresight to include pictures for people like me," I said to the dog nestled beside me. I couldn't translate half the words I saw. Only the pictures helped me determine the category of spell. "I bet this grimoire belonged to Ivy Rose, just like the wand."

PP3 lifted his head from the pillow on the sofa and I instinctively glanced at the door. Someone was here. The fact that the Yorkshire terrier didn't bark was a good sign. I didn't bother to wait for the knock. I set the grimoire on the coffee table and crossed the room to open the door.

"Calla?" The white-haired crone stood on my doorstep, her back slightly hunched.

The former High Priestess cracked a toothy smile. "Are you ready, daughter of the One True Witch?"

"Daughter?" I said. "Try great-great-great-whatever."

"It's an expression, duckling."

I leaned against the doorjamb. "What do you want me to be ready for?" If this was some sort of sales call for an anti-aging potion, the coven chose the wrong spokeswitch. Calla looked like she had one foot, an elbow, and an armpit in the grave.

The elderly witch brushed past me. "For your herbology lesson. Didn't your aunt tell you?"

"You're teaching me about plants?" I asked. I shut the door and trailed after her as she entered the kitchen. Unlike my aunt, Calla clearly didn't stand on ceremony.

The crone placed herself at the island and produced her wand. "Herbology has always been my specialty."

"But you're not coven appointed," I said. Although she was the former High Priestess, Calla was now only known as a crone. "Shouldn't someone else be doing this?"

Calla gave me a pointed look. "Your aunt asked me specifically. Should I tell her no?"

"I generally don't recommend it."

"Good, then we should get started," Calla said. "I have a dance lesson in ninety minutes and I need time to warm up. My limbs aren't what they used to be."

I squinted at her. "You take dance classes?"

She shrugged her bony shoulders. "I'm retired. What else am I going to do?"

I splayed my hands on the island countertop. "Well, since I kill everything within my wingspan, I'm not sure I'm the right witch to add to your roster."

"You haven't killed the roses outside," she said.

"An oversight," I replied. "There's still time."

Calla laughed. "Yes, time for you to master this skill. Very important for a witch of your caliber."

"I have a caliber?" I asked. "You obviously haven't talked to Hazel about me."

Calla flicked her pruned fingers in a dismissive gesture. "Runes. Bah! Anyone can get help reading runes."

I folded my arms. "Now we're talking. A witch after my own heart. So tell me, Calla, if you expect me to learn about plants, don't you think you should've brought a few?"

Her lip formed a satisfied curl as she aimed her wand at the countertop and uttered a Latin phrase I didn't recognize. A selection of potted plants appeared in two rows.

"Well, that's me told off," I said. I peered at the variety. "I hope we're starting basic because I have no plans to poison anyone…today."

"You're too hard on yourself," Calla said. "You've come late to your magic. No one expects you to be Hyacinth."

"Ha! Hyacinth expects me to be Hyacinth," I said. "And you can imagine how disappointed she's been."

"She remains ever hopeful that her line will remain strong. That's all. When you come from the most powerful line of witches and wizards in existence, you can easily succumb to the pressure."

"I succumb to the pressure of macaroni and cheese even after three days in my fridge, so I can imagine what it's like when the stakes are higher."

"Your aunt has her flaws, but she wields her power well overall," Calla said. "If she didn't, she would have been put in her place long ago."

Well, that was interesting. "Put in her place by whom? Aunt Hyacinth is the unofficial power center of this town." A fact that Sheriff Nash openly resented.

"The coven. The Council of Elders. The mayor." She ticked off the names on her hand.

"There's a mayor?"

Calla smirked. "How long have you lived here? You should pay closer attention."

"Since Aunt Hyacinth is a member of the Council of Elders, I think she'd manage to subdue them."

"You'd be surprised," Calla said. "They can be a tough bunch when they desire it."

"Yeah, I've met them." More than once. Marley liked when I referred to them as the cave dwellers, because that's where they held their secret meetings—in a cave by the ocean.

Calla crooked her finger, beckoning me closer. "Tell me if you can identify any of these."

I hovered over the rows of plants. I wasn't sure why I even gave the pretense of scrutinizing them. I couldn't distinguish a cactus from a eucalyptus. "Echinacea." A complete guess.

"Which one?" Her fingernails clicked expectantly on the hard surface.

I snapped to attention. "Seriously?"

"One of them is definitely Echinacea," she said.

"The...green one," I said.

She blew a raspberry. "You weren't kidding. You don't know a burdock from your buttock."

"Hey!" I objected.

Calla opened her cloak and began to hike up her tunic top.

"Whoa," I said, waving my hands. "Herbology doesn't involve one of those naked rituals, does it? Because I haven't exercised in weeks."

"Weeks?" Calla challenged.

"Months. Years. What's the difference?"

Calla produced a hip flask and smoothed her top back down. "I didn't get the sense that you were a prude," she said. "Not with all those boyfriends of yours."

"All those boyfriends?" I sputtered. "You make it sound like I've dated half the town."

"Even so, you have to think of it from the point of view of the other women in Starry Hollow. Two of the most eligible males in town have fallen prey to your questionable charms in a very short time. They would've pegged you for a witch even without your aunt's declaration."

I glared at her. "What's so questionable about my charms?"

The crone ignored the question. Instead she unscrewed the lid and took a swig. "That hit the spot." She smacked her lips and set the flask on the countertop.

"Is that some kind of potion for your old lady ailments?" I asked.

Callan regarded me curiously. "And which old lady ailments would those be?"

"I don't know. Rheumatism. That seems to be a biggie."

Calla threw back her head and cackled. "Sure. It's for rheumatism. Let's go with that."

I snatched the flask and sniffed it. "This smells like alcohol."

"What a coincidence," the crone said slyly.

"How do you expect to teach me about magical herbs if you're drunk?" I asked.

"I'm not drunk," Calla scoffed. "I take an occasional nip to keep me going and keep you interesting."

I gaped at her. "You are far more delightful one-on-one."

She smirked. "So I'm told." She took another drink before replacing the lid. "Let's begin. I need to report back to your aunt and she's going to want to hear that we were productive."

"I thought once she had a suitor, she'd relax a little," I grumbled.

Calla snorted. "She has years of ice to thaw. That won't happen overnight." She touched the third pot from the left in the first row. "This is Echinacea, by the way."

"In case I develop a cold?"

"In case you want to strengthen a spell," she replied. "It's often used as an add-on."

I studied the pinkish flower. "Give me an example."

"Where's your grimoire?" Calla asked. She surveyed the kitchen. "I don't suppose you keep one out here."

"No, I'll be right back." I hustled to the living room and plucked the old grimoire from the coffee table. PP3 tilted his head as if to say 'what now?' I gave him a quick scratch behind the ear before returning to the kitchen, where I dropped the well-worn book onto the countertop.

Calla's eyes rounded. "This is your grimoire?"

"No," I said. "Marley got it as a gift from Aunt Hyacinth, along with a wand. Family heirlooms, apparently."

Calla stroked the soft cover. "I don't think I've ever seen one as old as this." She glanced at me. "And yet she gave it to your daughter and not to you?"

I shrugged. "Fair enough. Marley is going to be a much better witch than I'll ever be."

"With your parents, I find that hard to believe." She flipped open the book and scanned the pages. "This is beautiful. I'll come back to teach you for the sheer pleasure of looking at it."

"You're getting distracted," I said.

She smiled. "Happens a lot at my age. You'll see."

"Do you happen to know anything about one of my ancestors called Ivy? This was her grimoire." From the state of the grimoire, though, I suspected that even Ivy was not the original owner.

Calla inhaled sharply. "Great Goddess of the Moon. I haven't heard her name in many years."

"You knew her?"

"Of her," Calla corrected me. "She was before my time."

"What do you know about her?" I asked.

"She was very powerful, even more so than your aunt," Calla said. "She ruled this area with an iron fist."

"She was the High Priestess?" I asked.

"For a time, until she was made to step down," Calla said.

"A Rose with a sordid past? Tell me more."

Calla stared at the grimoire, as though looking for answers there. "I wish I could remember. My memory isn't what it used to be, duckling."

"Maybe there's a spell in here for that." I inclined my head toward the grimoire.

"You're quirky," Calla said. "The coven could use a little more character. Everyone else is so perfect." She made a face. "Makes for very boring parties."

I regarded her. "You realize you just insulted me, right?"

She seemed unconcerned. "Who wants to be perfect?" She pointed to a spell. "Here's a good example for you to try. This one involves edelweiss. It makes you invisible for a brief period of time. Adding Echinacea strengthens the spell in the event that anyone tries to counteract it."

Invisibility sounded like fun. "Did you happen to bring any edelweiss?"

Calla wagged a finger at me. "You're going to be a good time, Yarrow."

"It's Ember." Yarrow was apparently my birth name, the one the family-at-large had insisted I be given.

"Right. Ember." She pushed a small pot toward me. It contained a small sprig of white flowers. "Your edelweiss is ready and waiting. An excellent first lesson, I think."

"You don't think it's too advanced?" I queried.

"Only one way to find out."

"You're much more lenient than Hazel and Marigold," I said. "They act like I'm on the verge of a magical breakdown if I tilt my wand too many degrees to the right."

Calla cackled softly. "They're both uptight. Comes with the age. They'll mellow out in a few more years."

"In that case, can I delay my lessons with them for a few more years?"

The crone pushed the grimoire over to me. "Can you read this?"

"I've been working on it," I said. "It's a mishmash of languages so it's slow. The pictures help." I had no doubt Marley would have it all figured out before I made it through the index.

She flicked her wand over the page and said, "*Illuminâre.*" The words melted into English.

My jaw unhinged. "Are you kidding? What do I need runecraft for with a spell like that?"

"Shortcuts are not for everyday use," Calla said. "There is power in knowledge. I may not remember everything I've learned in my long life, but I know that much is true."

I read the short spell. "You want me to perform this one by myself?"

"I'm curious to see how you do."

I sighed. "Fine, but I make no promises."

"That's what I told my first two husbands." Her scratchy laugh was infectious and I heard myself laughing too.

I retrieved a mortar and pestle from the cupboard. My heart grew heavy as I carried them to the counter. The mortar and pestle had been a gift from the sheriff. He'd seen them in a shop and bought them for me on a whim.

"Problem?" Calla inquired.

"No problem," I said. "Just good old-fashioned guilt rising to the surface." I crushed a few of the edelweiss petals along with my guilty feelings and added a dash of Echinacea. Then I performed the chant, using the original Latin. I was guaranteed to send myself to another realm if I tried to read the spell out loud in English.

A tingling sensation spread throughout my body. I examined my arms and legs. Still intact.

"Well done, Ember," the crone said.

"Am I invisible?" Other than the tingling sensation, I felt the same.

"You are."

I danced around the kitchen like I was auditioning for a show on the Vegas strip.

"You're dancing, aren't you?"

I froze. "No," I said slowly.

She laughed. "Liar. It's fine. Everybody does their first time. Invisibility can be freeing."

"How long does it take to wear off?" I asked.

"The Echinacea will extend it somewhat, but I'd say only a few minutes, based on the amount you made."

"I should carry this around in a packet," I said. "It could come in handy at Aunt Hyacinth's dinner parties."

Calla pilfered a small drawstring bag from her pocket. "Use this. I always carry a few packets of herbs with me, in case of emergency."

"Which ones?"

She opened her cloak and I glimpsed several packets pinned to the inside of the fabric. She looked like the oldest drug dealer in Starry Hollow. "The green bag is a protection spell. The yellow bag is for psychic powers. Mind-reading to be specific."

"What do you need protection from?" I asked. "Is it like a spray can of mace?"

Her eyes twinkled. "Not quite that kind of protection."

The realization hit me. "Oh! Ew!" Forget about STDs. I didn't want to think about the crone in a sexual situation of any kind.

Calla cackled. "You won't be saying 'ew' in a few years."

"More than a few, thank you very much," I countered. By

the time Calla finished reviewing two more plants with me, the invisibility spell wore off. I dumped the remainder of the spell in the packet she gave me and secured the drawstring. "Thanks, Calla. This was more entertaining than I expected."

She tucked her flask back where it belonged. "Same. I'll give your aunt the glowing report."

"She'll think I bribed you."

"With what? A crone like me has everything she'll ever need." She patted the part of her cloak where her flask was hidden.

"Next time consider sharing," I said.

She grimaced. "Calla doesn't swap saliva with anyone unless he pays for dinner first."

"Fine, then next time bring two flasks."

The crone nodded her white head. "Done."

CHAPTER EIGHT

DANA ELLSWORTH'S office reminded me of a whimsical city loft with an open-plan layout, exposed pipes, and pops of bold color. No surprise that she worked for a marketing company. The receptionist was positioned in the eye of the storm. She wore glasses in the shape of a cat's eye and a leopard print dress.

"I'm going to go out on a limb and say wereleopard," I whispered to Deputy Bolan.

He glanced at the receptionist and chuckled. "I don't know. Maybe a dwarf."

"Not with that body," I said. Even in a seated position, I could tell the receptionist had the kind of body that made Florian look twice.

"Can't say I notice." The leprechaun shot me a quizzical look. "On that note, why do *you* notice?"

I shrugged. "Doesn't mean I want to marry her. A woman's body is beautiful in all shapes and sizes, but that's an enviable one right there."

His brow lifted. "Ah, I get it. You're coveting."

"I guess, but I don't begrudge her what she's got."

The deputy softened. "You don't need to worry, Rose. You look good."

I half smiled. "I thought you didn't notice women's bodies."

He groaned. "I was forced to notice yours thanks to your budding romance with the sheriff."

"He talked about my body?" That didn't sound like the discreet sheriff.

"Not in a bad way," the deputy replied. "He would just make offhand comments, like 'doesn't Rose look pretty in that dress' or 'doesn't Rose have the best legs you've ever seen'?"

Unshed tears burned my eyes. "Okay, Deputy. That's enough," I said quietly. Images of the sheriff from the interrogation flashed in my mind. He'd looked like he wanted to be in bed with the covers pulled over his head.

"Sorry," the deputy mumbled.

We approached the receptionist's desk and I let the leprechaun take the lead. His head was barely visible above the tall desk. "I'm Deputy Bolan and this is my colleague, Ember Rose. We'd like to see Dana Ellsworth, please."

The receptionist smiled demurely and I was pretty sure I heard the distinct sound of purring. "I'll see if Miss Ellsworth is available." She picked up the phone.

"We can see she's available," I said, pointing to the loft above. "She's right there on her computer."

The receptionist tilted up her chin to confirm my statement. "So she is." She pressed a button. "Hello, Miss Ellsworth. I'm sending two visitors up to see you now. Deputy Bolan and his purrr-ty girlfriend."

I fought my gag reflex at the way she pronounced 'pretty.' She was suddenly the living embodiment of every kitten poster in the doctor's office I'd ever seen.

The leprechaun began to object to the description of us,

but the receptionist was still focused on the call. "I'll be sure to let them know." She hung up the phone and offered the hint of a smile. "Miss Ellsworth said to go ahead up. Shall I escort you to the stairway?"

"We can show ourselves, thanks," the deputy said. "It's right behind you."

The receptionist showed a gleaming set of white teeth. If she said 'pur-fect' I was going to hurl. "Have a good day," she said, and I unclenched.

Deputy Bolan and I trudged up the metal staircase and met Dana at her desk. The vampire appeared to be in the middle of a project, with designs scattered across her desk and piled up on the floor beside her stool. Petite with corn-silk hair and wide brown eyes, she was blessed with the smooth, ageless skin of her kind.

"Is this about that skinny-dipping incident," Dana began, "because I swear I thought it was totally cool with the owner?"

The deputy and I exchanged glances. "Um, no," the leprechaun replied. "You'll have to tell us that story another time. Do you have a private space where we can talk?"

Dana's expression shifted to one of concern. "Is it my dog? Did something happen to Kiki? Those squirrels torment the hell out of her."

Deputy Bolan made a calming gesture. "You must have a conference room here somewhere."

Dana pointed behind us. "The fishbowl is that way." She vacated the stool and we followed her past a row of other workstations. Her heels clicked loudly on the wooden floor. She stopped in front of a room where three of the walls were made entirely of glass, hence the fishbowl.

"We can talk in here," she said, and crossed the threshold.

The table and chairs were in keeping with the style of the interior. Metal flashed from every angle. I sat on an end chair and it was every bit as uncomfortable as it looked. Dana perched on the edge of the sideboard.

"We understand you know Tatiana…" The deputy didn't get to finish his sentence. At the mere mention of Tatiana, Dana's eyes blazed with anger.

"What did that train wreck of a fairy do now?" she snapped. Her eyes rounded. "Wait. You're the local deputy. Does that mean she's in town?" She clenched her fists. "Terrific. I'm already stressed about a client meeting and now I have to deal with the fact that my former best friend is here to wreak havoc."

"So you haven't seen her?" Deputy Bolan asked.

Dana slid down from the sideboard. "I haven't seen that winged backstabber since she hightailed it out of here with her loser boyfriend years ago." Her gaze flitted from the deputy to me. "So she's really in town?"

"She was," I said.

"She's gone already?" Dana queried. "What happened? Did she rob some poor sucker blind before she flew off?"

"She didn't rob anyone," the deputy said. "She's dead."

Dana steadied herself against the sideboard. "Dead? Not undead like me, right? You mean real dead?"

"Real dead," the deputy confirmed.

The vampire's lips melted into a malevolent smile. "Good. Whatever happened, I'm sure she deserved it."

I tried to contain my shock at her reaction. She could at least feign a touch of sadness for her former friend. "You mentioned that the two of you were best friends at one time," I said. Clearly, not anymore.

"Yeah, until she decided to get it on with my fiancé behind my back," Dana said. "That sort of behavior generally puts the kibosh on a friendship, you know?"

The deputy stood beside my chair. I assumed he didn't want to sit so that he wasn't any shorter. Right now we were about eye level. "Did you confront Tatiana at the time?" he asked.

"I confronted both of them, fangs and all." She popped out her pointy teeth for good measure. "I drew blood. Mostly Jake's, but I got a few decent digs in with Tatiana too, before Jake went full wolf and ruined my advantage. He's strong enough when he's in human form."

"Jake's a werewolf?" I queried.

"I know, I know. Vampires and werewolves are supposed to be eternal enemies," Dana said. "Mythos shmythos. Well, we're enemies now, but at the time we were completely drawn to each other, probably because the relationship was so frowned upon. I thought we would live happily ever after." She paused. "I was a moron."

"Was Tatiana supportive of the relationship?" I asked. Was there a chance Tatiana had tried to do her friend a favor by showing Jake's true nature before the wedding? Based on my knowledge of the fairy, the chances were slim, but still. She was dead and I wanted a better understanding of her. If for no other reason than it was the best way to pinpoint her killer.

"Of course she was. She thought Jake was hot," Dana said. "Then again, she thought every male on two legs was hot." She paused. "Even four legs, for that matter."

"Sounds like Tatiana was very open-minded," I said.

Dana glowered at me. "She was a sparkly slut."

Okay then. "What about Jake?" I asked. "Any chance he's been in touch with Tatiana?" Inwardly, I cringed at my use of the word 'touch.'

"I have no clue and I don't care," Dana said. "Jake can rot in Heaven for all I care."

"I think you mean Hell," the deputy said.

She scoffed. "A guy like Jake would do well for himself in

Hell. No, I mean Heaven. All that goodness. He'd die a slow and painful death."

"Well, technically if he were in Heaven he'd already be dead," Deputy Bolan said.

Dana silenced him with a menacing look. "Go and talk to Jake if you want, but do me a favor. If they've been in contact, I don't want to know. I put that ordeal behind me a long time ago and I don't want to relive it now. I have a successful graphic design job, and a great group of friends who would never betray me. The undead life is sweet." She kissed her fingers like she'd finished creating a culinary masterpiece.

"No boyfriend or fiancé?" I asked.

Dana pinned me with a resentful look. "No, but there's plenty of time. I'm immortal, remember?"

"Anyone since Jake?" I asked.

She pretended to examine her lengthy black fingernails. "No one worth mentioning."

Hmm. So not really over the ordeal at all.

"One more question, Miss Ellsworth," Deputy Bolan said. "Where were you on Monday between the hours of nine and three?"

"Here at the office, same as always," Dana said. "Unlike some unscrupulous fairies and wayward werewolves, I don't shirk my responsibilities."

Her bitterness seemed as eternal as her life was.

"Thanks for your time," the deputy said.

"No problem," she replied. "Thanks for the good news. I might run out for a blood orange milkshake to celebrate. Care to join me?" She cocked an eyebrow at the leprechaun.

"We have a dead fairy and no one in custody," Deputy Bolan replied. "We're not celebrating anything today."

Dana offered a pert shrug. "Your loss."

"My husband would disagree," the leprechaun said.

As we left the fishbowl, I placed a hand on the leprechaun's tiny shoulder. "If you have any powers of persuasion with Granger, please don't let him end up like that."

"From your lips to the gods' ears," the deputy said.

I was in the middle of an intense daydream involving Alec, me, and a vibrating broomstick when I was interrupted by a knock at the door. I bolted to my feet, heat emanating from my entire body. PP3 stirred at the end of the sofa but didn't move.

"Don't worry, guard dog," I said. "I'll answer it." We both knew who it was anyway. I opened the door and flashed a deranged smile. "Welcome to the madhouse."

"I'm glad you finally chose to acknowledge it." Hazel strode into the cottage, gripping a purple bag I'd never seen before.

"Do a little shopping recently?" I asked.

She hefted the bag onto the dining table. "It was a gift, if you must know."

My brow creased. "Someone bought you a gift? What happened?" I pictured an innocent family approaching her and asking if she'd show off her juggling skills. With her red curls and big red lips, Hazel looked like a descendant of the One True Clown. If Halloween were a thing in Starry Hollow, she wouldn't even need a costume.

The Mistress-of-Runecraft scowled. "Why does something have to happen in order for me to receive a gift?"

I shrugged and joined her at the table. "So who's the benefactor?"

She stroked the bag's soft material. "If you must know, it's a gift from my sister. She lives abroad with her family and sent it as a memento from her trip to Bon Mage."

"That's a shop?"

72

"No, a small city." She scratched her cheek. "It's not too far from your human city of Paris. Much older, though. Brimming with ancient magic."

I inclined my head. "I guess that purple bag is magical then."

"It has its perks." She opened the bag and reached inside for the runecraft book I referred to as the Big Book of Scribbles. She bit her lip as she continued to rummage through the bag.

"Don't go too deep," I said, "because I'm not rescuing you from the underworld if you fall in."

Hazel ignored my remark. "Ah, here it is." She pulled out the book and placed it on the table with a thump. She must have registered my disappointed expression because she said, "Did you think I might have left it behind?"

"One can remain hopeful."

She opened the book to the page after our last lesson. "We can pick up right where we left off."

"Yippee," I said, with only the tiniest hint of sarcasm.

Okay, maybe it was loaded with sarcasm.

She set a blank paper in front of me and handed me a fancy black marker. "I'd like to see improvement in your flourishes today. I've given you ample time to practice."

"What can I say, Hazel? I'm not the artistic one in my family."

"Speaking of Marley," the crazed clown said, "how is she enjoying her new school?" She hugged herself. "I absolutely cherished my time at the academy."

"All that homework and discipline," I said. "I can imagine." Egads, Hazel had probably been the worst brown-noser in school. "Marley seems really happy there. I feel like her world is finally starting to come together now that she has magic."

"I never doubted it for a second," Hazel said. "She reeks of excellence. It's no wonder your aunt chose to bequeath the wand and grimoire to Marley."

"And what do I reek of?" I held up a hand. "Wait, don't answer that." An image of the portrait in the Black Cloak Academy Hall sprang to mind. "Do you know anything about our ancestor? The one that's framed on the wall at the academy? She was holding the wand that Aunt Hyacinth gave to Marley."

Hazel brightened. "Oh, you must mean Ivy."

I nodded enthusiastically. "Yes, that's her. Same white-blond hair as the rest of the bunch."

"Yes, that hair color is a stunning feature. Too bad you didn't manage to inherit it." She didn't sound particularly sorry.

"What's her story?" I asked. "Calla said Ivy was the High Priestess at one point, but was forced to step down. She didn't recall the particulars."

"To be honest, I don't know much about her," Hazel admitted. "Perhaps you should ask your aunt. She's the one in possession of the witch's personal effects."

"I'm sure she inherited them, same as everything else," I said. "It doesn't mean she's privy to details about the witch's life." I made a mental note to ask Delphine Winter, the local librarian. As a member of the coven, she was bound to know something about Ivy.

"Well, I've heard rumors, of course," Hazel said, "but I'm hardly an expert."

My head swiveled toward her. "What kind of rumors?"

Hazel lowered her gaze. "Oh, I shouldn't tell tales out of school."

"We're not out of school," I insisted. I patted the book on the table. "This is exactly the place where you should tell tales."

Hazel hesitated. "I don't know. Your aunt would take her

wand to my knuckles if she knew I was saying something I shouldn't."

"I highly doubt Aunt Hyacinth would resort to old-fashioned schoolroom discipline. Her methods are far more subtle."

Hazel winced. "True. She only needs to give me a certain look and my insides quiver with fear."

"She has talent, I'll give her that."

"Unlike you," Hazel said. "Now show me that you've learned something." She tapped impatiently on the table.

I managed a few strokes with the fancy black marker. "There. Satisfied?"

Hazel hovered over me. "You can't be serious. Is that the best you can do? It looks like your canine companion dipped his paws in an inkwell and walked across the page."

I glanced up to meet the crazed clown's critical gaze. "Aren't you supposed to be supportive and encouraging?"

"Since when?" Hazel scoffed. "Your aunt doesn't ask me to be supportive. She asks me to teach you magic. I'm not about to give you a gold star for halfhearted efforts."

"Halfhearted?" I repeated. I gesticulated dramatically to the page on the table. "That's blood, sweat, and tears right there."

"I require none of those things," Hazel said. "Only correctly drawn runes."

"Calla is way more relaxed than you," I said. I heard the note of taunting in my voice, but I didn't care.

Hazel aimed her wand and my chair pulled out from under me. I dropped to the floor, flat on my butt.

"Ouch." I got back on my feet and rubbed my sore bottom. "No need for violence."

"Says the Jersey girl."

"Violence doesn't suit you, Hazel," I said. "It looks much better on me."

The door flew open and Raoul stumbled in. He looked even worse than the last time. Bonkers flew in after him, landing on the cottage floor with a thud. Her right wing was torn and her hair was askew. I was relieved Marley wasn't home to see the state of her.

"Great Goddess," Hazel said. "Look at you both."

I scooped up Bonkers off the floor and examined her injuries. "We need a healer."

What about me? Raoul asked, thrusting out his paws.

"We'll get to you next," I assured him. Marley would never forgive me if something happened to Bonkers because of my suggestion.

"I have some healing abilities," Hazel said. She bustled over and took Bonkers from my hands.

"Since when?" I asked.

Hazel gave me a firm look. "I'm a far more competent witch than you give me credit for."

"Competent in being annoying, yes," I said. "Competent in healing. Not so much."

Hazel glared at me. "Do you want me to heal this creature or not?"

I put my hands on my hips. "You'd deny her treatment because of my salty attitude? Some healer you are."

Hazel's hands began to glow and I jumped back. She smiled in satisfaction. "It's fun to surprise you."

Hurry up, Raoul whined. *I want my turn to be coddled.*

"What happened?" I demanded. "You were at the dump?"

The crow, Raoul said. *What do you think?*

"This is ridiculous," I said. "He can't be that tough. He's a crow, for Elvis's sake, not a wolf."

"Maybe you should go down to the dump and take care of him then," Hazel said.

I thought of all the times Sheriff Nash teased me about being a broomstick mama, or as humans call it—a helicopter mom. "I can't. This is the kind of thing Raoul needs to resolve on his own."

"It's not a schoolyard scuffle," Hazel said.

"No, it's a junkyard scuffle," I shot back. "I don't belong in the middle of it."

The raccoon lowered his head in abject disappointment and I felt a twinge of guilt. *You're right. I've gotten by my whole life without a support system. I can do this on my own.*

His words stung. I knew what it was like to operate without a net. To get through each day knowing that the only one I could count on was me. Starry Hollow had changed all that for me. Why couldn't I change all that for Raoul? He was, after all, my familiar. That made him family.

"Okay, I'll help you," I said.

His raccoon face jerked up. *You will?*

"Your bully is my bully," I said. "We're a team, Raoul. We'll handle him together." Out of the corner of my eye, I noticed Hazel's smug smile.

Raoul lifted his paw to high-five me and I was careful not to get scratched by his sharp claws. *Got any food? A guy can get pretty hungry after an altercation.*

"I don't think you need an excuse to be hungry," I said.

No, but I was working the sympathy angle. Did it work? He eyed me hopefully.

I motioned for him to enter the kitchen. "There are cookies in the tin."

He hesitated. *Um, just out of curiosity…*

"Marley made them."

His relief was evident. *I hope there's milk. Can't have cookies without milk.*

I rolled my eyes. "Don't push your luck."

He disappeared into the kitchen before I could change my mind. When I turned back to the Big Book of Scribbles, Hazel's amused expression caught my eye. "What?"

"Nothing," she said quickly. "Sometimes you remind me so much of your aunt and other times…"

I frowned. "Other times what?"

She sucked in a breath. "And other times I feel as though I could actually like you."

CHAPTER NINE

I KNEW something was amiss the moment I walked into the office at *Vox Populi*. Tanya and Bentley wore matching concerned expressions and no one bothered to greet me. Bentley didn't even offer an insult.

"What's going on?" I asked.

"Your little green friend is back there with Alec," Bentley said.

My pulse began to race. "Deputy Bolan?"

"I told him unequivocally that Alec would never harm a hair on Tatiana's head, but he ignored me." Tanya dabbed at her eyes with a sparkling handkerchief.

"He's not supposed to conduct interviews without me." I stormed off to give the leprechaun a piece of my mind. We were supposed to be working as a team. Interrogating my boyfriend without warning was completely unfair.

I heard Alec's voice through the closed door. "Am I to be charged with anything?"

"That's to be determined," Deputy Bolan replied. "*Should* I be charging you with something?"

"You want to," Alec said. "I can hear that thought loudly and clearly."

"No mind reading! That's against the law."

"It actually isn't," Alec said. "You simply need better defensive measures."

I threw open the door, ready to throttle the deputy. "Back away from the vampire."

Alec sat behind his desk, looking like his usual calm and cool self. Deputy Bolan stood by the top left corner of the desk. He straightened when he saw me. It didn't help him look taller, but I imagine it made him *feel* taller.

"Rose, I was told not to expect you until later in the day," the deputy said.

I wagged a finger at him. "You're not supposed to be doing this without me."

The leprechaun jabbed a green finger in Alec's direction. "He's your boyfriend. You can't be privy to the interrogation."

"He's not officially my boyfriend yet," I said. "So I can be here."

Deputy Bolan seemed momentarily confused. "He's not?"

"I'm not?" Alec echoed.

"He hasn't fulfilled his obligation yet," I said.

"And what obligation would that be, Rose?" Deputy Bolan asked.

"That's personal," I said.

"If you want to witness this interview, in complete silence I might add, then tell me why he's not officially your boyfriend."

I crossed my arms. "Because we haven't gone to couples counseling yet." I needed to make the appointment, but the counselor I'd originally wanted didn't handle couples.

I expected the leprechaun to laugh or mock me in some way. Instead, he gave me a respectful nod. "Smart." He pointed to a chair. "Now sit and don't say a word." He motioned to his head. "And no mind reading either. I can tell when you're doing it, so don't even try. Your eyes go goopy."

"Goopy?" I repeated. "Is that a word?"

The leprechaun's beady eyes bugged out. "I'm doing this as a favor. Don't make me regret it." He turned back to Alec. "Do you know why you're here?"

"I work here," Alec replied smoothly.

I stifled a laugh. Deputy Bolan looked ready to have a coronary.

"Fine. Do you know why *I'm* here?" he asked.

"Tatiana is dead," Alec said, his voice devoid of emotion. "You would like to know whether I killed her."

Deputy Bolan's eyes narrowed into slits. "Did you?"

"Certainly not." He adjusted his suit jacket.

Deputy Bolan sank into the chair next to mine. "Oh well, if you say so."

"Excellent," Alec said. "Am I free to return to my duties? It seems there might be a need for me to research couples counselors."

Deputy Bolan slapped his hand on the desk. "Of course not! How did you find out about her death?"

Alec didn't flinch. "Tanya, her aunt, works for me, as you saw when you came in," he said. "She was quite distraught. Until that moment, I wasn't aware that Tatiana was in town."

"She didn't come to see you?" he asked. "Try to get reacquainted with an old flame?"

Alec folded his hands on the desk. "If she did, she failed to leave a note."

"How did you feel when you heard the news?" Deputy Bolan asked.

I tensed slightly, awaiting his response.

"Surprised," Alec said.

The deputy inclined his head. "In what way?"

Alec rubbed his thumb on an invisible speck on the desk. "I suppose she seemed immortal to me. Like a vampire."

"Like you."

"Yes."

Deputy Bolan fixed him with an intense stare. "So you decided to test your theory?"

"Don't be absurd," Alec replied. "Tatiana was a fairy. I know perfectly well fairies aren't immortal."

"Do you still harbor resentment toward her?" Deputy Bolan asked.

"As you and your boss both know, I have since moved on."

Deputy Bolan snarled. I didn't think I'd ever seen a leprechaun snarl before. Why did Alec have to say that? It was the equivalent of slapping your opponent with a silk glove. I was glad Sheriff Nash wasn't present to hear it.

"Perhaps your timing is suspect," the deputy said.

Alec's smooth brow furrowed. "How so?"

"Out of the blue you decided to give Ember a chance," the leprechaun said. "Maybe you lured Tatiana here with the promise of a fake inheritance and then used Ember as a cover. Maybe you planned this a long time ago."

"In which case I could have stayed with Holly and accomplished the same goal," Alec replied. "It makes no sense to send Holly packing when she would have provided the same cover."

"Except you didn't send Holly packing," Deputy Bolan said. "She left you."

"Because she knew I had feelings for someone else," he replied.

"Everyone in Starry Hollow knew you had feelings for someone else," the deputy grumbled.

"Then this line of questioning is pointless," Alec said.

Deputy Bolan seemed to agree. He slouched in the chair. "You remember Dana Ellsworth, right?"

"Indeed. Someone else burned by Tatiana's treachery."

"She mentioned her ex-fiancé, Jake," the deputy said.

"Ah, yes. Jake Goode," Alec said, a glimmer of recognition in his eyes. "Another werewolf, as I recall. He owns Body By Jake."

"He's a fitness instructor?" Deputy Bolan asked.

"Allegedly," Alec said. "It's my understanding that he's more interested in showing off his own physique."

Deputy Bolan rubbed his chin. "Sounds like he's definitely worth a visit."

I laughed. "I'll bet."

"Where were you on Monday between the hours of nine and three?" Deputy Bolan asked.

"In a meeting with the mayor," Alec said. "Feel free to corroborate it."

"There really is a mayor," I said.

"The whole time?" the deputy asked. "Nine to three?"

"No, I was here first thing in the morning with my staff. After that, I went for a massage, then I met with the mayor."

"And the massage was where?" the deputy asked.

"Glitter Me This," he said. "You can speak to Rosie to verify."

"Is she any good?" Deputy Bolan asked. He rolled his neck from side to side. "I've had a kink in my neck for days."

"She's excellent," Alec said. "I wouldn't bother otherwise."

"I didn't know you went for massages," I said.

"Well, now you do," Alec said simply.

"This is the kind of thing we need to discuss in counseling," I said. "I should know this about you."

"It's only a massage, Ember," he said.

"But what else aren't you telling me?" I said, feeling hurt.

Deputy Bolan slapped his hands on his thighs. "My work here is done. I'll be in touch." He left the office, leaving Alec and I staring at each other.

"Are you truly upset about this?" Alec asked.

"It's part of your communication skills," I said. "I feel like you hide things that don't need to be hidden. It makes you seem shady, whether you mean to be or not."

"It didn't occur to me that you need to know every appointment I make."

"I don't," I insisted. "It isn't about keeping tabs on you."

He arched an eyebrow. "Are you quite sure?"

"Yes." My tone was emphatic. I needed him to understand that this wasn't a jealousy issue. "I'm going to schedule our appointment as soon as I get home. I'll text you the details."

He gazed at me with a tender expression. "I look forward to it."

"You do?"

"I want this relationship to be successful, Ember," he said. "I have every intention of following your lead."

I smiled. "Stop picturing me on your desk. I said I'm not doing it." I paused. "Today."

He laughed. "Like I said, I have every intention of following your lead."

And I couldn't wait to be his captain.

The Master-in-Familiar Arts marched us into the woods behind Rose Cottage. I'd tried to explain to Ian that I was very busy working on Tatiana's murder investigation, but the wizard was having none of it. Raoul seemed pleased that Ian had stood his ground, probably because he liked the attention Ian gave him.

"Before we get to what I'm sure will be a fascinating lesson in the nocturnal habits of dumpster divers, can we discuss a problem of a personal nature?" I asked.

Your breath? Raoul interjected.

Ian chuckled. "Oh, aren't you a clever one?" The wizard

had already performed the spell that allowed him to access both Raoul's thoughts and mine during the lesson. It was easier than relying on me to translate the raccoon's thoughts, especially because I was prone to not necessarily relay the exact statement.

"Raoul is having an issue with a bully down at the dump," I said. "I've offered to help him take care of the situation."

Ian tapped his foot. "And?"

"And do you think I'd be doing the right thing?" I asked. "My gut says yes, but then I hear the sheriff's judgy voice telling me to let Raoul deal with it himself. That he won't learn how to navigate these situations if I step in and save him."

"Interesting," the wizard.

"Is it?" I said. "Seems like a normal witch-familiar issue to me. Similar to the parental bond."

I am not your kid, Raoul said, horrified.

"No," I agreed. "Not a kid. More like my grown son with a college degree in underwater basket weaving that lives in my basement and eats cold pizza while he plays computer games all day."

I do like cold pizza.

"I don't mean that the story itself is interesting," Ian said. "I mean the fact that you still care what Sheriff Nash thinks of you. You're no longer together, correct?"

I could feel the blood flowing to my cheeks. "Correct."

"Then what does it matter whether he approves of your involvement? If your gut tells you to step in, then step in."

Raoul grunted his agreement.

"What does Alec have to say about it?" Ian asked.

I paused. "I don't know. I haven't asked him."

"Interesting," Ian said again.

"No, it's really not," I said.

I agree, Raoul said. *Alec is really not*.

85

I faced my familiar. "What? I thought you liked him."

Ian steepled his fingers together. "Oh my. Perhaps we should save this conversation for after the lesson. I do have other matters to attend to today." He sniffed loudly, his perpetual congestion getting the better of him.

Raoul and I crossed our arms in sync. "What's on the agenda today?" I asked.

"I thought today we could explore extending your magic to include your familiar," Ian said.

I blinked. "Extending my magic? What does that mean?"

He means sharing, Raoul said. *A foreign concept to only children like you.*

My hands stuck to my hips. "I'll remember you said that the next time you raid my kitchen." I turned back to Ian. "Are you talking about transferring my warmth to him, that kind of thing? Because I thought we covered that."

"No, I'm talking about extending a spell to include him," Ian explained. "So if you do a spell to…"

"Make myself invisible," I interrupted, remembering my lesson with Calla. "Then I can make Raoul invisible too?"

The raccoon rubbed his paws together. *Ooh, me likey. Imagine the possibilities.*

Ian's brow furrowed. "I don't know that the two of you need the power of invisibility for any reason, but yes, that is precisely what I mean."

I patted my pocket and felt the lump of the edelweiss and Echinacea packet still there. "We can experiment with it right now. I have the herbs with me."

Ian contemplated the suggestion. "I think it's best if we do a spell that allows me to see you both."

"Afraid we'll ditch you in the woods by yourself?" I asked.

Raoul snickered. *We would totally do that.*

I laughed. "I know, right?"

The wizard maintained his composure. "How about a

simple levitation spell?" he suggested. "You do the spell on yourself and I'll explain how to include your familiar."

I planted my feet in the ready position and held my wand. "Sounds good."

"Take his paw," Ian instructed.

With my free hand, I curled my fingers around the raccoon's paw. "Do we have to hold hands?"

Raoul cut me a sharp look. *What's the problem? Afraid of cooties?*

"Well, you do spend more time in a garbage heap than in the bath, but no. I only want to know if the spell will work in another way in case I can't hold your paw for some reason."

"Touching your familiar is the most expeditious way to perform the spell," Ian said. "It makes sense to start with that."

No touching the tail, Raoul warned. *I don't care what kind of danger we're in. The tail is sacred.*

"Sacred?" I echoed. "Since when?"

The raccoon slapped his tail on the ground. *I just don't like to be tail-handled, okay? Deal with it.*

I rolled my eyes. "Sheesh, message received."

"Now you'll perform the usual levitation spell," Ian continued, "except you tack on another term at the end. *Includere familiaris.*"

I focused my will and summoned my magic. Energy pulsed through me as I concentrated on the spell. "*Surgo.*" My feet rose from the ground and I was just about to lose my grip on Raoul when I added, "*Includere familiaris.*"

The raccoon joined me about two feet above the ground.

That's all you got? Raoul asked. His gaze dropped to the ground. *I can jump higher than this even when I'm not avoiding bear traps.*

"But you can't stay there," I said. "You fall right back to

the ground. There's that little thing called gravity that prevents you from staying airborne."

He wobbled slightly, finding it hard to keep his balance. *I'm impressed that you managed it on the first try. I was expecting to shoot into the sky like a rocket.*

I fixed with my hard stare. "There's still time." I lowered us back to the ground and Ian clapped merrily.

"Excellent performance, Ember." The wizard seemed exceptionally pleased. I guess he expected us to shoot into the sky like rockets, too.

"What's the practical reason for this?" I asked. "It's not like I need him to levitate with me unless we're avoiding lava." Which was unlikely.

Or bear traps, Raoul reminded me.

"What about including him in a protective bubble?" Ian suggested. "You sometimes find yourself in a precarious situation. What if you needed to protect your familiar as well?"

I cast a quick glance at Raoul. "It would depend on my mood that day."

Raoul huffed. *Some family you turned out to be.*

I threw my head back and groaned. "Oh, stop. You know perfectly well that I'd protect you. I'm not a monster."

Raoul dragged his paw through the dirt. *You don't seem anxious to protect me from the crow.*

"It isn't that she doesn't want to," Ian said. "She was conflicted for good reason, but I believe she's come around to the idea."

"Thank you, Ian," I said. "Yes, I have."

Raoul's dark eyes bore into mine. Today?

"Not today. I have Marley's initiation party at Thornhold later. I can't possibly show up smelling like I lathered myself with aging lettuce and moldy tomatoes."

I disagree. Bottle that scent and you're on to a winner, Raoul said. He tapped his claw against his chin. *Note to self. Gather lettuce and tomato at the dump. I'll call it Eau De Salade.*

"Will I see you at Thornhold for Marley's big party, Ian?" I asked. I knew from Simon that the guest list was extensive. From what I gathered, my aunt had basically invited the entire coven as well as the Council of Elders and other key paranormals in Starry Hollow.

"Oh, yes indeed," the wizard said. "No one in their right mind would turn down an invitation to Thornhold."

"I guess not." Although I hoped the sheriff wasn't in his right mind because I had no doubt he was on the guest list. As much as my aunt sneered at the pack, she wouldn't dare leave off key figures in the community. With Alec as my plus one, however, the combination could be a recipe for disaster. I pushed the thought to the back of my mind. The party was days away and, right now, I was no closer to solving Tatiana's murder today than I was yesterday. Deputy Bolan and I were going to have to up our game if we expected to handle this without the sheriff's involvement.

"Everyone wants to be in your aunt's good graces," Ian continued.

I don't see why, Raoul said. *It's not like she's going to write them into her will because they came to all the parties they were invited to.*

"One can dream," Ian said good-naturedly.

The mention of wills gave me pause. Deputy Bolan and I still hadn't identified Tatiana's mysterious benefactor—the main purpose of her visit. What if the inheritance was somehow connected to her murder? It was time to find out.

CHAPTER TEN

I SENT a text to Deputy Bolan from my car in the parking lot of the sheriff's office. Five minutes later, the leprechaun tapped on my window, startling me. "Sheesh," I said, rolling down the window. "Save those ninja skills for the field, Deputy."

"You sent me a text to meet you out here. How is this a surprise?"

"I thought you might take longer." I almost said 'because of your leprechaun legs,' but I decided against it. We were making an effort to get along.

"Are we covert agents now, Rose?" he asked. "What's with the secrecy?"

"I don't want to run into the sheriff," I admitted. "We need to find out about this inheritance. No one seems to know who died and named Tatiana as a beneficiary. It's nagging me."

"Good point. We can run a check on recent death records and see if anyone is connected to Tatiana," Deputy Bolan suggested.

"But Tanya would know if it's a family member, and that's

the only obvious link," I replied. "I guess we can generate a list of names and show them to Tanya and our suspects. See if anyone can identify a likely benefactor."

"It doesn't make sense that Tatiana wouldn't name the decedent," the deputy said. "She was the type to shout it from the rooftop."

"Agreed." Unless it had been a secret relationship. Even with that, though, Tatiana wouldn't likely honor the secret once the other party was dead. She had no shame. The only other possibility was that Tatiana didn't know the identity of the benefactor, but if that were true, then what would be the reason for anonymity?

"Give me a few minutes to grab the list and then we'll go from there." Deputy Bolan shuffled back to the building. I played on my phone while I waited.

"Loitering outside the sheriff's office? That's got to be a violation of some kind." The sheriff's voice jolted me and I dropped my phone. He leaned down to peer through my open window.

"I'm waiting for Deputy Bolan," I said.

Sheriff Nash forced a grin. "Two peas in a pod now, aren't you?"

"We just want to make things easier for you," I said.

His expression clouded over. "No need to treat me with kid gloves, Rose. I'm a big wolf. I can take it."

I straightened. "I'm not being precious. I just know that Tatiana's death..." I trailed off. "I'd like us to be normal with each other. I'd want to help with this investigation no matter what our relationship status is."

He stood erect. "Nothing normal about us, Rose. There never was. I'll see you around." He turned on his heel and headed for the building before I had a chance to say anything else.

Ugh. This was awful. I hated being at odds with him. I

knew this would be the likely outcome, but I still didn't like it. Granger was important to me. Just because I'd chosen to make a start with Alec didn't mean I wanted to excise the werewolf from my life. He'd been a welcome fixture.

Deputy Bolan scuttled back to the car with a piece of paper. "I think we should take this list to the library and see if we can cross-check names with Tatiana."

I looked at him askance. "The library? But you're at the sheriff's office. Aren't you in a better position to get this information?"

The leprechaun tapped his nose. "Between you, me, and the fey lantern, she's my secret weapon. You'd be surprised what Delphine Winter can do."

I wouldn't, actually. I knew the pretty witch was far more capable than her quiet demeanor let on. "I haven't seen her in a while." Ever since she and my cousin Florian had broken up, I'd seen less and less of her, which was a shame because Marley and I were very fond of the librarian. We were fond of anyone who loved books.

"No time like the present," he said. "I'll drive this time, though. You tailgate too much."

"I do not," I replied in a huff.

"You ride so close you can see their speedometer from your driver's seat." He paused. "Plus you play too much Billy Joel."

I reeled back. "What?" His words did not compute. "There is no such thing as too much Billy Joel."

"The songs are depressing," the deputy continued. "That *Piano Man* sounds like a musical mid-life crisis. *We Didn't Start the Fire*? Seriously? And don't get me started on Bruce Springsteen."

I sputtered a string of obscenities before pointing an angry finger at him. "Don't you dare disrespect the Boss."

Deputy Bolan laughed. "That's his nickname. More like

the Bomb. And I mean the kind that's not good, not the ironic kind."

"At least I don't need a booster seat to see over the steering wheel," I said.

The leprechaun glared at me. "That's a low blow, Rose."

"How else could I reach you down there?"

He gasped.

"You're wasting time out there," I said. "Just get in my car. I promise to play *Danny Boy*, or whatever Irish music you lay claim to."

Begrudgingly, he climbed into the passenger seat and buckled his seatbelt. I drove us over to the library, blasting *Come On Eileen*. The band was Irish. That had to count for something.

We entered the library arguing about whether Lucky Charms was a racist cereal. It wasn't hard to guess the deputy's feelings on the subject.

"Look at the two of you, working together. I love it!" Delphine's cheerful voice drifted over to us from behind the counter. The leprechaun and I exchanged guilty looks.

"It's sort of a necessity," Deputy Bolan said.

Delphine scrunched her nose. "Did something happen to the sheriff? Is he ill?"

The deputy and I approached the counter. "No," I said. "He's been sidelined for the moment, at least for this investigation."

Delphine lowered her voice. "Why? What happened?"

"Did you hear about the fairy that drowned in a pool?" Deputy Bolan asked.

Delphine's expression crumpled. "Good Goddess, no. How awful."

"She was murdered," I said.

"And because Sheriff Nash has a prior relationship with the deceased," the deputy continued, "we thought it best to take over the investigation to avoid the appearance of impropriety."

"Yes, that makes sense," Delphine said. "Not that the sheriff is capable of anything like that. Can you imagine?"

"So it's our understanding that Tatiana came back to Starry Hollow to collect an inheritance," Deputy Bolan explained, "but no one seems to know the name of the deceased or what the inheritance was."

"Deputy Bolan has a list of recently deceased residents and we're trying to find out if any of them might be connected to Tatiana in any way."

The deputy unfolded the paper he'd printed at the office. "If you could work your magic on any of these names, it would be a big help."

For some reason, I assumed he meant metaphorical magic, which was pretty dumb considering she was a witch. Delphine scanned the list. "Let's do this somewhere more private."

"Whatever you need," the deputy said.

We trailed Delphine to a room at the back of the library. I expected to enter an office, but it was a Spartan room with hardwood floors and shelves lined with candles and jars. Delphine plucked a piece of white chalk from a shelf and drew a circle on the floor. She sat cross-legged in the middle and motioned to me.

"You'll be helpful, Ember," she said. "Sit with me."

I glanced at the deputy with uncertainty. He held up his hands. "Hey, Rose. You do what you've got to do. I'm only a leprechaun."

I joined Delphine in the circle. She had the list between us. "Hold my hands and then ask your question," she said.

I did as instructed and she began to chant. Candles lit without warning and I bit back a smile when Deputy Bolan jumped in response. I watched in awe as names began to get crossed off the list by an invisible hand. She stopped chanting and released my hands.

"Are we done?" I asked.

Delphine frowned. "Yes."

"What is it?" I asked.

"Only one of these names have a connection to Tatiana," the witch replied. "I've drawn on a blank on every other name." Sure enough, every name save one was crossed off the list.

"We only need one name," the deputy said. "Who is it?"

I peered at the list. "Kiev Petrov." I looked at Deputy Bolan. "Did you know him?"

"I did," Delphine said. "He was a regular here. Vampire. He particularly liked the medieval history section."

"A vampire?" I said. "Do you know how he died?"

"He'd been ill for quite some time," Delphine said. "I heard from one of the healers that Kiev had opted to end his life rather than continue to suffer. You should talk to his son, Oleg. They were very close. They owned an antiquities shop together."

"I guess we need to go see Oleg," I said. "Maybe he can explain the connection to Tatiana."

"I'll be right back," the leprechaun said. "Leave that chalk circle just in case. I'm going to call the office and make sure we didn't miss any names." He slipped out of the room.

This was a good time to broach the subject of Ivy with Delphine. Before I could open my mouth, she gave me a shy look. "I hate to ask, but how's Florian?" she asked.

"His usual man-child self," I replied.

"Not dating anyone special?" she asked.

"Not since you," I said. "You know Florian. He doesn't want what he considers the trappings of marriage and kids. Not yet anyway. How about you? Any suitors?"

A blush crept into her cheeks. "Maybe."

"Really?" I would be one hundred percent delighted if Delphine met someone. I knew how badly she'd wanted things to work out with Florian. Even Aunt Hyacinth had been on board with the librarian due to her association with the coven.

Delphine glanced around nervously before whispering in my ear, "Wren Stanton-Summer."

My eyes nearly popped out of their sockets. "Are you kidding?"

"No, why?" She became anxious. "Am I making another poor choice?"

"Not at all," I said. "I think he's fantastic." I paused. "Don't tell him I said that, though. I have a reputation to maintain. How did this happen?"

"We got to talking at the last coven meeting," she said. "He asked me to go broomstick flying and we had the most amazing time." She clasped her hands together. "We've been out a couple more times since then, but we've tried to keep it quiet."

"Why?" I asked. "I would think everyone would be pleased with two members of the coven finding each other." Unlike me and my unsavory taste in werewolves and vampires.

"We want to be sure this is going somewhere," Delphine said. "I felt so foolish after Florian." She stared at the floor and sighed. "I thought I could change him."

"His mother is still convinced she can change him," I said, "so you're not alone."

"I'm a little worried that Wren is more like Florian than I think," Delphine admitted.

I balked. "No way. Wren is nothing like Florian. For starters, he acts like a grownup." Most of the time.

"He hasn't settled down, though," Delphine said. "I'm not sure he's ready. What if he only thinks he is?"

I considered the question. "I don't know, Delphine. It's always a risk, isn't it? That things won't work out."

She nodded. "I just don't know if I can go through that again."

I knew exactly what 'that' was—the heartbreak. "But if you think Wren is worth it…"

She perked up. "I do. He's so sweet, Ember." She smiled. "Very considerate. He's never late and he's always interested in my opinion."

"Plus he's hot," I said. "Can't forget that part."

"He *is h*ot," Deputy Bolan interjected. I hadn't heard him come back into the room. "In fact, I have a free pass for him."

I shot him a quizzical look. "You have a free pass for Wren?"

The leprechaun nodded his little head.

Delphine blinked. "A free pass for what?"

"If the opportunity presented itself and Wren was game, then it wouldn't be considered cheating if the good deputy here took a walk on the wild side with a wizard." I broke into a smile. "You *shall* pass."

Delphine's hand flew to her chest. "Oh."

Deputy Bolan produced a small laminated list from his pocket. "See. I have three names."

I grabbed the list before he could put it away. "Only you would have it laminated," I said. "Wren is number one. How about that?"

He snatched back the list and tucked it into his pocket. "Anyway, the point is that I approve of you dating him, Delphine."

The witch didn't seem sure how to respond. She was still processing the fact that the leprechaun had a list.

"I have another question for you," I said. "It's about a portrait I saw in the hallway of the Black Cloak Academy."

Delphine lit up at the mention of the school. "Oh, how is Marley adjusting? I bet she loves it there."

"She's doing well, thanks," I replied. "When we toured the building, we noticed a portrait of one of our ancestors. Ivy. Have you heard of her?"

Delphine appeared thoughtful. "No, I don't believe I have."

"You have a whole section here on Starry Hollow and its residents," I said. "Is there a good resource you can think of that would include her?"

"Let me see if I can narrow down a few books for you," the witch said.

"Thanks, that would be great."

"Why don't you ask your aunt?" the deputy asked. "She probably has a family tree painted on a wall somewhere in that mansion of hers."

I chewed my lip, not sure how to answer. "I don't think I'll get the full story from her. Aunt Hyacinth has a tendency to tell stories that suit her agenda."

"And what agenda is that?" Deputy Bolan asked.

"Depends," I replied. "She's giving Marley this witch's wand and grimoire. I know there are reasons why these are deemed special by my aunt. I want to know what they are from an unbiased source."

"I hate to admit it, Rose, but they might just make a reporter out of you yet," the deputy declared.

"Gee, thanks."

Delphine gestured for me to follow her. "We need to go upstairs."

"We're done here, right?" the deputy said.

"We didn't miss any other names?" I queried.

He shook his head. "Nope. Just the one lead to follow."

"Well, we also have Body By Jake to interview," I said.

He scratched his head. "Yeah, let's get to Oleg first. If he can tell us about his father's connection to Tatiana, we might not need to see Jake."

"I would think you'd be disappointed by that," I said. "Hot fitness instructor."

"Sounds more up your alley," the deputy said. "Unless you meet Oleg and decide a vampire is better." He snapped his fingers. "Oh, wait. You've already done that."

I simmered. "That's enough, Deputy."

We parted ways and Delphine and I headed upstairs to the local history section. She pulled a few books from the shelf and dumped them on a nearby table.

"We can start with these," she said. "Check the index for her name first."

I sat at the table and opened the first book.

"I'm just curious," Delphine said, "is there any reason why she'd give the wand and grimoire to Marley and not to you or one of her daughters?"

"I've had the same thought," I said. "I really don't know. I figure if I learn this witch's story, that might explain it."

"Here's a reference to her," Delphine said. She flipped to the page listed in the index. "Oh, wow."

My brow lifted. "What?"

Delphine snapped the book closed. "Nothing."

"Nothing? You can't react like that and then tell me it's nothing." I tried to wrench the book from her grip.

"I'm sure some of this is exaggerated," Delphine said.

"I thought this was the unbiased account," I argued. I gave her a stern look. "Give me the book, Delphine, or I'll tell Wren that you've already named all five of your future children."

She shrank back in horror. "You wouldn't!"

I wriggled my fingers. "The book."

She slid the book over to me and I turned to the page. "Ivy, a descendant of the One True Witch, was stripped of her magic after…" I stopped reading aloud. It was too terrible. That must've been the reason she was forced to step down as High Priestess.

Delphine hung her head. "I'm sorry, Ember."

"Why would Aunt Hyacinth want Marley to have such powerful tools?" I said, to no one in particular. "If this witch couldn't handle them, what makes her think Marley can?"

"Maybe that's the reason she bypassed her daughters," Delphine said. "She was worried about the impact on them."

"Then what does that mean? Marley is expendable?" The idea was overwhelming. Aunt Hyacinth couldn't possibly feel that way. She adored Marley. Everyone did.

And yet.

"Can I check out this book?" I asked.

Delphine nodded. "Take it. I'll sign it out for you."

I hugged the book to my chest. I didn't care how busy I was with the investigation. I'd make time to get to the bottom of this. My daughter was my top priority. If Ivy's sordid past was linked to her wand or her grimoire, I was bound and determined to make sure that Marley didn't suffer the same fate.

CHAPTER ELEVEN

THE ANTIQUITIES SHOP reminded me of a carefully curated museum. The exterior was a Gothic-style house made of gray stone with arched windows on the top floor and a steeply gabled roof. The interior rooms were organized according to its antiquities and works of art. The first room off the entryway included only paintings—portraits of European vampires wearing somber expressions, Roman stone mosaics, and modern oil on canvas of a coven meeting. The second room we entered was full of masks and skulls. A painted demon mask carved from wood. A green stone skull of an elf. Each item was wholly unique.

A sleek vampire strode into the room. His custom suit was reminiscent of Alec, but the similarities ended there. Oleg's hair was dark and curly and he stood no taller than me.

"I see the Mask of a Young Werewolf has caught your attention," Oleg said. "You have a keen eye." He glanced down at the deputy. "Should I get you a step stool to afford you a better view?"

Deputy Bolan scowled and I bit back a smile. "We're not

here to acquire any items, although I did admire that Portrait of a Leprechaun's Luck in the other room," he said.

Oleg's smile broadened. "Apologies for the impertinent remark."

"We're here on official business," I said.

"And what business is that?" Oleg asked. "A beautiful woman like you...Let me guess." He observed me closely. "Your patron has sent you to add to his collection."

Deputy Bolan snorted. "He thinks you're a kept woman."

"Try again," I replied, keeping my gaze pinned on the vampire. I felt his mind reach out to probe mine. My shield was up, thanks to my experience with Alec. I knew the leprechaun would be able to withstand the invasion as well, especially after Alec's remark about the deputy's weak defensive measures.

Oleg locked his hands behind his back. "You are not here to admire my inventory."

"Afraid not," I said. "We have questions about your father."

Oleg lowered his head. "May he rest peacefully in the arms of the devil."

"Were you privy to the contents of your father's will?" I asked.

"Of course," he said. "I am the sole heir."

"Sole? No one else received anything from the estate?" Deputy Bolan asked.

"Absolutely not," Oleg said. "The estate reverted to me in its entirety."

Interesting. "Are you familiar with a fairy named Tatiana?" I asked.

Oleg flashed his fangs. "What has that ruinous viper done now?"

"I guess that's a yes," I said.

"What was your father's connection to her?" the deputy

asked. "Is there any reason he would have left her something in his will?"

Oleg laughed uproariously. "I promise you, that is an unequivocal no. My father would never have left so much as a worthless trinket to that fairy."

"What makes you so certain?" I asked.

"She swindled us out of several items before she fled town," he said bitterly. "A bronze cross staff and an ivory spear to name two. Highly valuable items."

Well, that was the connection that Delphine picked up on. Theft of Kiev's antiquities.

"How long ago was that?" I asked.

"A fair number of years have passed," Oleg admitted.

"And yet you recall the exact items and their value?" I asked.

"One does not forget such a transgression," the vampire said.

"Nor forgive," I added.

"Certainly not," Oleg said. "Would you? It upset my father greatly. It was not long after that when we received his diagnosis."

"How did she manage such a feat?" Deputy Bolan asked. He gestured to the protective ward that shimmered in front of the masks. "You've obviously taken security measures here."

Oleg seemed hesitant to answer.

"She played one of you," I said. "Or both."

The vampire ducked his head. "She deceived me, that is true. Is that what this is about? At long last, have our items been recovered?"

"Did you report them stolen at the time?" I asked.

"How could I?" Oleg replied. "To be outwitted by a common fairy—it was humiliating for both of us." His voice dropped to a whisper. "I have long blocked the memory of her from my mind."

"Then you haven't seen her since her return to Starry Hollow?" Deputy Bolan asked.

Oleg snapped to attention. "Her return? When?"

His reaction seemed genuine, but I couldn't be too sure. I knew how well a practiced vampire could conceal his real feelings.

"Earlier this week," the deputy said.

The vampire slid his jeweled hands into his pockets. "She is here," he said softly, more to himself. "Tatiana is back."

"Have you been in contact with her since she left?" the deputy asked.

Oleg shook his dark curls. "Only once, not long after she left. It was not a very pleasant conversation."

No doubt. "You threatened her?" I asked.

"Begged. Threatened. Swore." Oleg laughed uneasily. "I was in such a state. I had never been so easily seduced. I didn't handle it well."

"You're not alone in that," I said.

"I imagine not," Oleg said. "She was too good to be a novice." He paused. "So why are you here?"

Deputy Bolan and I exchanged glances. Now seemed like a good time to come clean.

"Tatiana is dead," I said. "She came back to Starry Hollow and it seems that someone decided to exact their revenge."

Oleg didn't flinch. "I cannot say I'm surprised. She must have developed quite the list of enemies."

"Let's just say she won't be missed," Deputy Bolan said.

Oleg's gaze lingered on a mask on a nearby pedestal. It had two faces—one on either side. "She made a fool of me, yes, but I did not kill her. I can't say I wouldn't have if given the opportunity, though." He shifted his focus to the deputy. "Tell me, please. How did she die? Was it painful?"

"She drowned in a swimming pool," the leprechaun replied.

"Drowning is known to be a horrible way to die," Oleg mused. "A most violent death." His lips twitched, fighting a pleased smile.

"If you can think of anyone else who might have had a reason to murder her, don't hesitate to call," I said.

"I certainly will." The vampire stroked the dual-sided mask. "Should you come across the items she stole from me, I would appreciate a follow-up call," Oleg said. "Though I would be shocked if she kept them. Tatiana was an opportunist, and not remotely sentimental."

"No problem," Deputy Bolan said. His phone buzzed and he glanced at the screen.

Oleg gave me an appraising look. "And if you see anything of interest here, don't hesitate to come back. I'll be more than happy to attend to your needs."

I smiled. "I certainly will. My boyfriend would love it here. He has his own collection of antiquities at home."

"Is that so?" Oleg seemed intrigued. "Perhaps I've sold him a few pieces then. What's his name?"

"Alec Hale," I replied.

Oleg paled slightly. "Yes, of course I know Alec. Everyone does." He frowned. "Including Tatiana, if I recall correctly."

"We've ruled him out," Deputy Bolan said.

I jerked my head to look at him. "We have? When?"

The deputy waved his phone. "Just now. Apparently, the examiner found traces of werewolf fur attached to Tatiana's wings that he missed the first time around."

"In her wings?" I repeated.

"That fur gets everywhere," Deputy Bolan said. "I'm surprised you haven't noticed."

"I have a Yorkshire terrier," I said. "That's the only dog hair I usually see." A horrible thought occurred to me. "Can you run the fur through a database and match it to a specific werewolf, like a DNA test?"

"No," the deputy replied, "but I'll have the sheriff hand over a sample of his, so the lab can compare and see if they match."

I held my breath. If they didn't match, then we could rule him out. Fingers crossed.

Oleg inclined his head. "I suppose I am cleared, as well as Mr. Hale. Best of luck. I'd like to know who the culprit is, once you've uncovered the truth, so that I may congratulate him or her."

I didn't know how to respond in the face of such calm and cool vitriol. "We'll do our best."

"The wreath is so pretty," Aster said. "Make sure you fasten it to her hair."

"I know, I know," I said. "If the wind blows hard enough, it'll blow straight into the ocean." I stood in front of my daughter in her bedroom as Aster and Linnea helped me prepare Marley's induction ceremony ensemble. Marley and I had clipped a few roses from the garden to add to the wreath of small white flowers. A little pop of color never hurt anybody.

"Do we make the wind blow?" Marley asked. "Is that part of the ceremony?"

"You would think," Linnea replied. "There's always some-body who wants to play the role of Mother Nature. The coven is full of divas."

"I love that the ceremony is outside," Marley said.

"You've always been a nature girl," I said. "It was just hard to embrace that in a cramped New Jersey apartment."

Marley's eyes sparkled. "I can't believe this is happening.

I'm going to be a member of the Silver Moon coven, just like you."

I brushed a few stray hairs off her forehead. "Not just like me. Better."

"I'm glad your mother backed down on the solo ceremony," I said to my cousins. "I think Marley would've felt awkward on her own." Aunt Hyacinth had wanted a special ceremony just for Marley because she was a descendant of the One True Witch, but Marley and I objected to preferential treatment. Marley wanted to be inducted with the rest of the new members.

"I wish we could have convinced her to do the joint ceremony with the wizards," Marley said.

"Change is slow to come to the coven," Aster said. "For now, the witches have their own ceremony, as do the wizards."

"But wizards will be there?" Marley asked, smoothing the front of her white shift dress.

"Yes, Florian will be there," I said. I knew perfectly well that she wanted her favorite cousin present for the ceremony. "In fact, he'll be here any minute." He was in charge of transportation.

"And Sterling will be there," Aster added. "Everyone is very excited for you, Marley. This is a huge milestone."

"It's like a dream." Marley wiggled her toes. "Without shoes."

"I know, right?" I said. "Seems risky. Hazards of the forest are everywhere. Pine needles, cones, thorns, a sharp stick. The dangers are endless."

"You survived the experience," Linnea said with a trace of amusement. "I'm sure Marley will fare just as well."

A knock on the front door signaled it was show time. Marley gave PP3 a kiss on the nose before heading downstairs. Florian waited outside the cottage in the silver cloak reserved for special occasions. Marley's unicorn stood amidst three white horses—Bell, Book, and Candle.

"Firefly," Marley said happily. She hurried over to her unicorn.

"One of the perks of holding ceremonies in the forest," Florian said. "No vehicles."

Florian mounted Book. Linnea climbed on Bell and Aster and I stood next to Candle.

"You realize I'm no better at getting on a horse today than the last time," I said.

"Yes, but now you can use your own magic to mount her," Aster said.

I thought of the levitation spell that I'd used during Ian's lesson. "I can!" I used my wand to perform the spell and my feet lifted off the ground as my body rose in the air. Maneuvering myself sideways onto the horse was awkward but I managed.

I was pleased to note that Marley climbed on Firefly's back with no trouble at all. She certainly didn't inherit the grace gene from me.

"Everyone ready?" Florian asked.

"Let's go," Marley cried.

My fingers dug into the poor horse's neck as we entered the forest. One of these days I'd be more relaxed on a horse. Maybe.

I spotted the circle of large standing stones first. Then the rest of the clearing came into view. Witches in white dresses and wizards in silver cloaks milled around the stones, waiting for all the participants. Aunt Hyacinth beamed when she noticed our arrival. She stood with Iris Sandstone, the High Priestess. Iris wore a floor-length white dress and a silver crown with a moon. Her silver hair was in its usual braid that extended to her bottom.

Florian helped Marley down from her unicorn and

someone else escorted the animals away from the clearing until the conclusion of the ceremony.

"I feel like a celebrity," Marley whispered. "This is my red carpet moment. It's too bad Alec can't be here."

"This is definitely a vampire-free zone tonight," I said. Although during my induction ceremony, we were briefly invaded by Wyatt's werewolf pack. Linnea was *not* a happy camper to see her ex-husband running naked through the standing stones.

Magnus Destry strode over to greet us. "And another Rose is welcomed into the fold. A momentous evening for your family as well as the coven." The severe-looking High Priest shook Marley's hand. "I have no doubt you'll be the jewel in their crown."

"A warm Silver Moon welcome, Marley," Aunt Hyacinth said, sweeping through the circle. "You might want to adjust your wreath. We'll be starting in just a moment."

Marley's hand flew absently to her head. "Is it crooked?"

"Looks fine to me," I said.

"A few millimeters up on the left side will do the trick," my aunt said. She continued past us to speak to the other new members and their families.

"Millimeters?" Marley queried.

"Here let me get my measuring tape," I said. I pretended to reach into my pocket. "Just ignore her. You're representing the family, so she has this strange notion that you should be perfect."

"I'm glad you don't feel that way," Marley said.

I pinched her cheek. "How could I? You have me for a mother. You're starting at a disadvantage."

Marley giggled. "You're ridiculous."

The forest darkened and I realized the sun had set. Time to begin.

"Coven, take your places, please," Iris said. "New members stand together in front of me."

Everyone moved to their respective positions. I took my place between Linnea and Aster. Marley waved to me from her spot in the circle. She looked so grownup that I found myself misty-eyed.

Iris turned to the only wizard in a black cloak, the understudy to the High Priest. "Summoner," she said in a commanding voice. He lifted his blackthorn staff and aimed it at the circle. Flames burst into existence.

"O' wondrous Goddess of the Moon," Iris began. "Tonight we welcome our newest members to the coven. We thank you for the generosity that you have shown in bestowing us with such gifted witches."

"Thank you, Goddess of the Moon," we chanted. A gust of wind blew through the circle and knocked Marley's wreath askew. Oh boy. Aunt Hyacinth was probably itching to fix it. No chance she'd dive across the flames to do it; she'd end up in the healer's office with no eyebrows.

The High Priestess produced a silver wand and touched the flames. She proceeded to walk straight through the fire in the middle of the stone circle to reach the new witches. Even though it wasn't my first time witnessing this spectacle, a gasp still escaped me.

"Marley, we welcome you to the Silver Moon coven. You have our allegiance and our protection." She touched the tip of her wand to my daughter's forehead and drew a rune before moving on to the next witch. I peered through the flames, trying to decipher the rune. Out of the corner of my eye, I saw Hazel watching me intently. Great balls of scribbles. Now I was really under pressure. Ten bucks says she'd quiz me after the ceremony.

"We are honor bound to teach you the ways of the coven

and to assist you in managing your magic responsibly," Iris said, continuing the ceremony.

They were still trying their level best with me, not that I made it easy. Marley would be a dream witch for this coven. Smart, eager, responsible. She'd more than make up for my shortcomings.

I shifted my focus away from Hazel and caught sight of Gardenia, the coven scribe, typing away on her iPhone. The stout witch took copious notes on every coven event and reported them at the monthly meetings.

Iris lifted her arms high and began to chant. The rest of the coven followed suit. One of these days, I was going to catch up and memorize this stuff. For now, I was stuck feeling like I'd stumbled into the middle of a Zumba class taught in Swahili.

The Summoner retrieved his giant Aim 'n Flame and pointed the staff at the fire to extinguish the fire. Aunt Hyacinth made a beeline for Marley. I thought she was going to hug her. She did, but only after correcting the wreath on Marley's head. I hurried over to congratulate my daughter with a warm hug.

"How do you feel?" I asked, kissing her cheek.

"This was so cool," she replied. Her cheeks had to be sore from so much smiling. Still, she didn't complain. She was too happy.

Warm drinks were distributed and witches and wizards swarmed the newest members to welcome them personally. Calla and Zahara took turns embracing Marley.

"Calla is the Crone and Zahara is the Mother," I said. With her high cheekbones and lush strawberry blond waves, Zahara looked more like a supermodel than a Mother.

"Oh, I've been studying coven terminology," Marley said. "You're responsible for coordinating the rituals."

"Among other things," Zahara said. "It's nice to see you

already taking an interest."

"She's taken an interest ever since the moment three magical cousins showed up in our apartment," I said.

"We offer mentorships in the coven," Zahara said with a warm smile. "Perhaps you would enjoy being a mentee to one of the leaders."

Marley vibrated with excitement. "That would be awesome."

"Know who else would love that idea?" I said. "Aunt Hyacinth." I had no doubt my aunt expected Marley to be the future leader of the coven...or the town. Probably the universe if the pushy witch had her way.

"Attention, Silver Moon." Gardenia waved her phone in the air. The light of the screen was glaring now that the fire was out. "I have an announcement before everyone leaves. Hyacinth Rose-Muldoon would like to extend an invitation to the coven to celebrate Marley's induction at Thornhold on Saturday at eleven."

I heard sounds of approval around me.

"She would also like to remind everyone that the use of coasters is mandatory. No exceptions." Gardenia consulted her phone to check for any further details. "If you are caught setting a glass on furniture without said coaster, you will be escorted from the premises posthaste."

"Oh no. Not posthaste," Calla murmured. "Anything but that." She gave me a mischievous wink.

"It's all fun and games now until you find yourself in the driveway with Aunt Hyacinth's broomstick up your..."

"Mom!" Marley admonished me. "This is a nice ritual. Don't ruin it with your mouth."

I was pretty sure I could ruin it even without my mouth. I was talented in that way. "Sorry."

Calla cackled quietly. "Between you and Marley, the coven just got a lot more interesting."

CHAPTER TWELVE

MY LEFT EYE TWITCHED. I was more nervous about my first counseling session with Alec than I'd realized. At least he'd been ruled out as a suspect in Tatiana's murder. That would've made for an awkward session.

Alec was his typical flawless self. Perfect hair. Perfect suit. Plain perfect...except for the traumatizing emotional baggage he seemed to carry. No biggie.

The door opened and the counselor beckoned us inside. I had no idea what to expect. My only experience to date was with Marley and that was only recently. I'd certainly never been counseled as part of a couple. Karl and I were too young to consider such things, not that we'd needed it. We operated as many couples did following the birth of a child— on sleep-deprived autopilot.

I'd been planning to use Marley's therapist, but he recommended that I see someone else for couples. Apparently, adolescents were his specialty. He did, however, suggest Aimee Hillside.

"Don't be shy," Aimee said in a squeaky, high-pitched voice. Her smile was so glaringly bright that I fought the impulse to shield my eyes. "I know the first visit is a huge step."

I nudged Alec to his feet and we joined Aimee in her office. She sat in a chair and motioned to the two—

Swings?

"Um, you want us to sit in those?" I asked.

"I think not," Alec said.

"I find it helps my clients relax," Aimee told us. "Swinging is soothing, like being back in the womb."

"I don't want to be back in the womb," I said. "I like it out here."

Aimee wagged a finger at us and clucked her tongue. "My room. My rules."

I peeked at Alec. His expression remained blank. "I guess it can't hurt." Unless I fell backward off the swing, in which case, it would hurt a lot.

Alec reluctantly sat on the swing adjacent to mine. He kept his feet firmly planted on the floor. I, on other hand, decided to gain a bit of momentum.

"Nice work, Ember," Aimee said. "Tell me, Alec. How does it feel to watch Ember enjoying herself?"

Alec gave me a cursory glance. "I take great pleasure in it."

"Then why not join her?" Aimee asked. "You can see she's having fun, yet you can't seem to lift up your feet."

"Is this how counseling works?" Alec asked. "You criticize one party in an effort to make them do your bidding?"

Aimee smiled. "Is that what you think is happening right now?"

Alec observed me on the swing. "To be perfectly honest, I have no idea what's happening right now."

Aimee punched the air. "Honesty, that's a fantastic start! So how long have you two been together?" She crossed her ankles and made herself comfortable.

"We've actually just started dating," I admitted. "We've

known each other for a while though." I found the swing to be every bit as relaxing as Aimee suggested.

"I see," Aimee replied. "And you're trying to start off the relationship on the right foot?"

"Something like that," I said. "Alec has been...somewhat emotionally unavailable."

The vampire's cheek pulsed. "Miss Rose...Ember was dating someone else."

I jerked toward him, red-faced. "So were you!"

"And were you involved with each other during those relationships?" Aimee asked. She held up her hands. "This is a judgment free zone, by the way. So if you were exchanging love blossoms behind your partners' backs, you can tell me."

"No," I said automatically. And a big fat no to love blossoms, whatever that euphemism was supposed to mean. I'd deny it based on my rejection of the expression alone.

"We were not involved in any identifiable way," Alec replied.

I looked at him as my swing swished past him. "That sounds like a lawyer's answer." I faced Aimee. "We work together. I guess we were involved in that regard."

"That's not what I'm referring to," Alec said.

Aimee smiled encouragingly. "Go on then, Alec. Tell us what you mean." She opened her arms wide. "Remember, these four walls represent the safe zone."

Dear God. If she jumped up and started doing the safety dance, I was running for the hills.

Alec shifted uncomfortably on his swing. "Even during my time with Holly, I thought often of Ember." He paused to adjust his cufflinks. "Far too often, in fact. I couldn't escape her influence."

I barked a short laugh. "Influence? How did I influence you?"

Aimee shot me a reproachful look. "Let him speak, Ember. He's expressing himself. That's what we want."

I pretended to zip my lip. I was finding it hard to have a third party in the middle of this conversation, although I knew she was here to facilitate said conversation. Aimee was right—the goal was for Alec to communicate, so I needed to be quiet and let the vampire talk. At least I could swing in the meantime.

"It was quite obvious that I had, and continue to have, strong feelings for Ember," Alec continued.

Aimee gave an exaggerated nod to show she was listening. "And what prevented you from expressing or acting on those feelings?"

"My relationship with Holly," Alec said.

"So you met Ember when you were already with Holly?" Aimee asked.

Alec hesitated. "No."

"Then what about before Holly?" Aimee asked. "What prevented you from pursuing a relationship with Ember then?" She looked at me. "Were you with your boyfriend?" She inclined her head. "What's his name?"

"Granger," I said. No need to call him the sheriff, even in the 'safe zone.' "No, I wasn't with Granger when Alec and I met."

"Her aunt owns my newspaper, so I am technically in her employ," Alec said.

"My aunt is very powerful," I said. "And opinionated. She wants me to marry within the coven."

"And she will most certainly blame me for luring Ember away from that plan," Alec said.

Aimee leaned back in her chair. "So you avoided your feelings because Ember's aunt might disapprove?"

"Yes," Alec said in a crisp tone.

"No," Aimee replied.

"No?" I repeated. "You don't think she'd disapprove? Ha! You don't know my aunt. Her type of disapproval makes Gengis Khan look like Santa Claus."

Aimee kept her focus on Alec. "He's a vampire, one who's been around for a long time. He didn't avoid his feelings for you because of a witch, no matter how powerful and vengeful."

Alec slid the sole of his shoe back and forth on the floor. Not quite swinging but there was movement. "Then what are you suggesting?"

Aimee's broad smile returned. "That's what we're going to explore in the safe zone."

I slowed my swing. The rush was starting to make me dizzy. "Alec had a difficult relationship with a fairy." I opted not to mention Tatiana's murder. That wasn't the point of raising the subject.

"And do you think this difficulty may have had an adverse effect on Alec's attitude toward relationships?" Aimee asked.

I shrugged. "You'll have to ask him."

Aimee winked. "Good thing he's right here."

"Tatiana certainly eroded my trust," Alec offered. "She could also be cruel at times. You would say something personal...reveal a bit of yourself...and she'd find a way to use it against you later."

"Wow. I guess that made you clam up, huh?" Aimee said. "I sure wouldn't feel great about sharing with someone like that."

"She was manipulative," Alec continued. "She used magic to influence those in her sphere." He shook his head. "I had no interest in relationships after that."

"Until you met Holly," Aimee said.

"No, until I met Ember," he clarified.

"I see." Aimee scribbled a few notes.

"What are you writing?" I asked. I hopped off the swing

and tried to peer at the notepad. Aimee snatched it up and held it against her chest.

"There's no need for you to see my notes," Aimee said. "They're for me."

"So what? You're making a grocery list while we're pouring our hearts out to you?" I said.

"No, of course not." Aimee looked at me askance. "I'm making notes so I can properly assess the situation and prepare for our next session."

Alec reached forward and patted my arm. "It's fine, Ember. Let her have her notes." I moved back to the swing.

"So you had an interest in dating Ember when you met her?" Aimee asked.

"Yes, a very strong desire," Alec said. "I felt drawn to her immediately."

"Same," I said. "I mean, I found him a little scary, having never met a vampire before, but it was like there was a neon sign flashing above his head with an arrow."

"And what did that signify to you?" Aimee asked. "The flashing sign?"

"The universe was telling me that he's the guy I've been looking for," I said.

"So you were looking to meet someone?" Aimee asked.

"Not exactly," I said. "I'd already been married and I hadn't really been interested in dating since Karl died."

"Karl was your husband?"

"Yes," I said. "He's the father of my daughter, Marley."

"And how old is Marley?" Aimee asked.

"Eleven," I replied. I couldn't help but smile when I talked about her. "She just came into her magic, so it's been an exciting time at our place."

Aimee smiled back at me. "I can imagine." She shifted her focus to Alec. "Did the fact that Ember has a child by another man give you pause?"

"Certainly not," Alec said. "Marley is an absolute treasure."

Aimee held up her hands. "I have to ask. Not all males are comfortable in that situation."

"Marley adores Alec," I said. "She's been rooting for us this whole time."

"And what is it about Marley that you like, Alec?" Aimee asked. "Vampires like yourself aren't exactly known for bonding with human children." She paused. "Magical or otherwise."

Alec pondered the question. "Her innocence, I suppose. The fact she's Ember's daughter. Her love of books."

"You like books, too?" Aimee asked.

"He writes them," I said.

"Which genre?" Aimee asked.

"Fantasy," Alec replied.

"I see." Aimee scribbled more notes.

"What do you see?" I asked. "Share with the class."

Aimee set down her pen and addressed me. "That someone who is uncommunicative, avoidant, and emotionally unavailable chooses to spend much of his time in a fantasy world." She brightened. "I can certainly see why you're here."

Alec stiffened. "I simply enjoy creating worlds of my own."

"Worlds where you can dwell and not deal with reality," Aimee said. "Worlds where you control everything that happens and you're not risking anything. Got it."

Wow. That was some quick insight on Aimee's part. "I've read some of his books," I said. "They're very good."

"I'm sure they are," Aimee said. "He wants to spend time somewhere that he enjoys and is comfortable. He's not going to build a garbage world."

I snickered. Raoul would be all over a story about a garbage world.

"Our goal is to explore why you've chosen these defense mechanisms or what we also call coping skills."

"If they're coping skills, isn't that a good thing?" I asked.

"Not when they're unhealthy," Aimee said. "If Alec isn't communicating or engaging with the important players in his undead life, then it's a problem."

"My stories are a matter of creative expression," Alec said. "I'm not hiding in them."

"Are you sure about that?" I asked. "You wrote a character based on me, didn't you? Instead of having a relationship with real me, your hero had a relationship with fictional me. I mean, she was awesome—don't get me wrong—but you focused on her because it was easier." I looked at Aimee. "Am I right?"

"Do you often feel the need to be right?" Aimee asked.

Alec half smiled. "She prefers it to being wrong."

"We'll have to explore that another time because I'm afraid our session is over." Aimee tilted her head at Alec. "Maybe next time you could swing just a little bit? I think it will relax you."

"It'll take a lot more than a swing and a cheerful attitude to relax this guy," I said.

She set aside her notepad. "In that case, I'll bring my harmonica. Everybody loves a harmonica."

I didn't have to look at Alec to know that he was ready to bolt for the door. An orchestra. Maybe even a guitar. But there was no way a harmonica was the key to unwinding Alec.

We were barely out of the building when he took my hand. "I promise you that I am not trying to avoid counseling, but another professional is in order. It will be difficult enough to share my innermost thoughts. I must at least endeavor to retain my dignity in the process."

"Okay," I said.

He stopped walking and faced me. "Okay?"

"Yep." I brought his hand to my lips and kissed it. "This will be a bumpy road for us. I want us both to be as comfortable as possible. I don't want a sore butt, do you?"

His mouth quirked. "Depends on the reason."

I wrenched my hand away and groaned. "Way to ruin a nice moment, Hale."

Dana was right about one thing. Jake Goode was hot. The werewolf was in the middle of a weightlifting set when we arrived at the Body By Jake fitness center. A variety of cardio machines and weights were scattered throughout the room. Colorful fabric ribbons hung from the ceiling. I had no idea what they were used for—trapeze training? Whatever they were, they looked like the kind of fitness equipment that would kill me slowly and painfully.

"Hey, new customers," Jake said affably. He stepped away from the weights to greet us. "Always happy to see new bodies ready for sculpting."

Jake had a combination of Granger's swagger, Wyatt's cockiness, and Florian's gorgeous looks. I could absolutely understand the attraction. So could Deputy Bolan, apparently. He seemed unusually tongue-tied from the outset.

"Hello, Mr. Good-looking," he began and his tiny cheeks flamed. The combination of red and green made his face look like a Christmas decoration. He cleared his throat and started again. "Mr. Goode. I'm Deputy Bolan and this is my colleague, Ember Rose. Just my colleague. Nothing else. We barely like each other, if you want to know the truth."

Jake didn't even try to hide his amused grin. "Are you

being specific for your benefit or hers?" He observed me from head to toe. "Because I'm open to suggestions."

Great balls of…balls. The leprechaun and I would both be clutching our pearls right now had we been wearing them.

"We have a few questions," the deputy choked out.

"Yes, I'm one hundred percent real," Jake said. "Nothing surgical or enhanced." He patted his impressive bare pecs.

"Um, that's not the question," the deputy said. "I hate to ask, but would you mind…putting a shirt on?"

Jake flexed. "Can't handle Body by Jake?" Sweat glistened under the fey lights and I was fairly certain a drop of drool appeared in the corner of the deputy's small, pink mouth. I had a feeling his 'free pass' list was going to be rearranged this week.

"We're here to discuss a serious matter and clothes are better on than off," the deputy said.

Jake winked. "That's never been my experience, but whatever you say, Deputy. You're in charge."

Deputy Bolan puffed out his skinny chest. "Yes, I am."

Jake bent over and pulled a black T-shirt from the bag on the floor. "What's this serious matter? Another health and safety complaint?"

Another?

"We don't work for the healthy and safety board," I said.

"Good, because Martha Barr needs to get a grip," Jake said. "That harpy is not getting communal showers here, no matter how many lies she spreads about my business."

"She wants communal showers?" I asked.

Jake began to wipe down the fitness equipment. "She's three-times widowed and eager to date and seems to want the showers to act as a shortcut."

"Ew," the deputy and I said in unison.

Jake nodded. "Yeah, and you haven't even seen Martha."

"Well, we're here to talk about a different man-eater," the

deputy said. He surveyed the empty fitness center before continuing. "We'd like to know about your relationship with Tati…"

The leprechaun didn't even finish her full name. Jake held up a hand. "What are you trying to do? Send me back to therapy? We do *not* speak her name out loud in Body By Jake."

"What do you call her then?" I asked.

"Hellbeast," Jake replied. "Or Satan's Favorite Child. Elsa."

"Elsa?" I repeated. "How is that on par with the other nicknames?"

He raised an eyebrow. "Have you ever seen that movie with the frozen chick?" He shivered. "Ice queen."

"Didn't you cheat on your fiancée with her?" I asked. He seemed awfully angry for a guy who participated in the betrayal.

Jake's bicep bulged as he continued to wipe down the equipment and I found myself as distracted as Deputy Bolan. "Yeah, that was me. Hellbeast cost me my fiancée, my future, my respect. It was a terrible time. Took me a long time to move on."

I nudged Deputy Bolan out of his stupor. The leprechaun snapped back to reality. "Why did you cheat if Tatiana was so horrible?" he asked.

"It's not that simple." Jake pressed his full lips together. He seemed reluctant to say more.

"She's a gorgeous fairy," I said, careful not to reveal the news of her death. Not yet. "It makes sense that you were attracted to her."

Jake threw the cloth aside. "I wasn't attracted to her. In fact, I hated her. I hated that Dana could be friends with someone like that. All she did was cause trouble. I was so relieved when she finally left town. The damage was done by then, though." He paused and squinted at us. "Why are we talking about her anyway? What's going on? She's not back, is she?" He dragged a hand through his hair. "Oh gods. Please say no."

"She returned to Starry Hollow for a brief stay," the deputy said. "You didn't see her?"

"No way," Jake replied. "I'd run the opposite direction if I saw her." He let loose a low whistle. "Dana will freak out. Ha! Good."

"Good?" Deputy Bolan asked.

Jake's expression hardened. "Dana treated me like garbage after she called off the wedding. She didn't want to hear my side of the story."

"Put yourself in her shoes," I said. "I'm sure she was deeply upset."

"She went into typical vampire mode," Jake said. "I should've known better than to get involved with a fanger. My mother warned me, but I didn't listen."

"Dana is aware that Tatiana was in town," I said. "We spoke to her."

Surprise flickered in his eyes. "When? Why?"

"Because Tatiana's dead," I said. "Someone killed her."

Jake swallowed hard. "Here?"

"In her aunt's swimming pool," I said.

Jake laughed awkwardly. "Wouldn't surprise me that she could enrage someone that quickly, though. If you'd ever met her, you'd understand."

"If you hated her so much, why sleep with her?" the deputy asked.

Jake's nostrils flared. "If I tell you this, will you promise not to tell anyone?"

"It has to be part of the investigation," the deputy said, "but I won't spread it around."

Jake crossed his arms, making his biceps appear even bigger. "I didn't cheat on purpose."

"So you what...tripped and fell in?" Deputy Bolan asked.

"No! She used fairy magic on me. She convinced me I was in love with her."

"Why would she do that?" I asked. Not only to Jake, but to her best friend, Dana.

"Because she was insane," Jake practically yelled. "And selfish. She tried to seduce me once, when Dana was asleep after a party. I said no and she couldn't handle it, so she spelled me into sleeping with her. Dana caught us." His hands moved to his hips in anger. "To this day, I think Tatiana set that whole thing up. She made sure Dana found us. She wanted to hurt both of us."

"Why?" Deputy Bolan pressed.

Jake gave us a dark look. "Because that was her nature. To hurt others for her own amusement. She couldn't stand that I rejected her, that I preferred Dana to her. That was her revenge on both of us for choosing each other."

I thought about Dana's version of events. "Why didn't you tell Dana the truth? Maybe you could have salvaged the relationship."

"I tried once, but she didn't believe me," Jake said. "She just kept saying 'once a cheater, always a cheater' like it was some kind of enchantment. After that, I let it go. I didn't want word spreading that Jake Goode wasn't interested in bedding the hot ladies. I figured my engagement was over and I'd need my rep intact."

"Are you dating anyone now?" I asked.

He wiggled his eyebrows. "Why? You interested?"

"Not right now, thanks," I replied. "I've just extracted myself from my own love triangle."

"And not very gracefully either," the deputy said.

Jake guffawed. Not many people could guffaw in this world, but Jake Goode was apparently one of them. "I date, but it's easier to keep it low-key."

"Dana's still single, you know," I said. "It's been years since you broke up. Maybe there's a chance you could rekindle things."

Jake snorted. "We learned our lesson. Vampires and werewolves shouldn't mix. Everybody knows that."

"Seems more like bad fairies shouldn't mix with anyone," I said.

"The truth is I'm planning to leave town soon anyway," Jake said.

"You are?" the deputy asked. "I should advise you to wait until the conclusion of the investigation."

"Where are you headed?" I asked.

"I've decided to take Body By Jake national," he said. "I'm opening another location in Sleepy Junction and renting a condo there until it's up and running with management in place."

"That's great," I said. "Congratulations."

"Thanks." He seemed shy about the admission.

"Sleepy Junction is pretty far away," the deputy said. "What made you choose there?"

Jake grinned. "The fact that it's pretty far away. I'm tired of hearing my mother ask when I'm going to settle down. I want to live my life without so much pressure."

I offered my knuckles for a fist bump. "Right there with you on that one."

Jake bumped me as the door opened. "Hey, Melody. I'll be right with you." He winked at us. "In the meantime, Body By Jake is fully operational and open for business, if you know what I mean."

"I'm not sure," I said. "It's hard to decipher when you're so subtle."

Deputy Bolan smothered a laugh. "One more question. Where were you on Monday between the hours of nine and three?"

"Here," Jake said. "I had clients in and out most of the day. You can check the roster."

"Would you mind providing us with a copy of it?" the deputy asked.

"No problem." The werewolf waved to Melody. "Be right back." He hustled down a small corridor to an office and returned with a piece of paper. "Feel free to get in touch with any questions. I'm almost always here."

"One more thing," I said. "We need a sample of your fur."

Jake held out his muscular arms. "As you can see, it's not available at the moment."

"Head over to the sheriff's office as soon as you can and provide a sample," the deputy said. He took the paper. "The sooner you do, the sooner we can officially rule you out and you can make your plans for Sleepy Junction."

"No problem." Jake turned his attention to Melody. "Hey, babe. Sorry, I was busy with police business. That's hot, right?"

"You bet it is," Melody cooed.

Inwardly, I groaned. Somehow I wasn't convinced that Tatiana's fairy magic was the only reason that Jake strayed.

"I'm starving," Deputy Bolan said as we ventured back to the parking lot. "Do you want to grab a bite to eat and go over the notes?"

"Can't," I said. "Aunt Hyacinth has changed family dinner night to tonight because of Marley's party at the weekend. I need to get home and change."

"I should probably check on the sheriff," the leprechaun said. "I've sort of been avoiding him until we finish the investigation."

"Me, too," I said. "Well, I'm kind of avoiding him anyway."

"That's your best course of action, Rose," he said. "He needs time."

"Jake and Dana had time," I said, jerking my thumb over

my shoulder. "Didn't seem to matter. No time healing all wounds there."

We stopped next to the car. "The sheriff...He isn't like Jake or Dana," Deputy Bolan said. "He's upset, but he won't be bitter. Not for long. I've worked with him a long time. He's one of the best, but you know that."

"I do know that." I inhaled deeply. "It's my loss, Deputy. The truth is I never saw it any other way."

CHAPTER THIRTEEN

A WEEKDAY FAMILY dinner at Thornhold was decidedly more stressful than a Sunday dinner. Everyone was rushing to arrive on time, so as not to ruffle Aunt Hyacinth's feathers, but it only served to create a nervous energy at the table. I could tell my cousins were mentally calculating how long they needed to stay before they could go home and do the things they actually needed to do—because I was doing the exact same thing.

"Sterling sends his regrets, Mother," Aster said. "He had a dinner meeting tonight with an important client from out of town."

Aunt Hyacinth brought her cocktail glass to her lips. "I understand, darling. Family can't always come first."

Ooh. A subtle jab. Would Aster rise to the bait?

"I love the new curtains in your office," Aster said. "I saw them on my way in."

Ten points to Aster!

"Thank you," Aunt Hyacinth said. "Mrs. Babcock made them."

"Is there anything that brownie can't do?" I said.

"She can't make Bryn more likable," Hudson said. "Believe me, I've tried."

Bryn appeared to stomp on her brother's foot under the table and he yowled in response.

"Where's Aqua Man?" I asked, hoping to divert attention away from the squabbling siblings.

Everyone looked at me blankly, except Marley who giggled.

"I don't believe I know anyone by that name," my aunt replied.

I groaned in exasperation. "Your merman lover."

Aunt Hyacinth regarded me coolly. "We do not use such vulgar expressions at the dinner table, Yarrow."

"Ha!" Hudson said. "She used your real name."

"*Ember* is my real name," I said heatedly.

"And you know perfectly well that my *friend's* real name is Zale Murphy." Aunt Hyacinth rang the silver bell she reserved for summoning Simon.

The loyal servant materialized in the doorway as though by teleportation. "I am at your disposal."

"Have the cook add extra sprouts to Ember's plate," my aunt ordered.

"Straight away." Simon disappeared as quickly as he came.

"You wouldn't," I hissed.

She gave me a smug look. "I believe I just did." She swallowed a mouthful of her cocktail. "I think you know me better than to expect I'd invite a random stranger to a family dinner."

"Once you've made out with someone, you can hardly consider him a random stranger anymore," I said. I paused and cut a glance at Florian. "Well, maybe you can…"

"CPR is not the same as *making out*, as you so crassly put it," my aunt seethed. "He saved me from drowning."

"What's making out?" Aspen asked from his end of the table.

"We'll discuss it later," Aster told him quietly.

"So if I want a stranger to be my friend, I ask them to make out?" Ackley queried.

Aster turned to her other son. "I'll explain later."

"Sorry," I mouthed to Aster.

"You'll be pleased to know that I've invited Mr. Murphy to attend Marley's party this weekend," my aunt said. "I expect you to be on your best behavior."

"Why would you expect that?" I asked.

Florian chuckled beside me.

"Alec will also be joining us this weekend, I presume," my aunt said.

"Yes," I replied. "He's looking forward to it."

"How's that going?" Aster asked. "Are you two finally official?"

"I've been wondering that myself," Aunt Hyacinth said. She gave me a pointed look. It didn't matter that she expected me to run my romantic prospects past her first. That would *never* happen, even if she threatened to boot me out of Rose Cottage. I refused to live under her iron-fisted rule.

"Sort of," I said. "We have some hoops we need to jump through first, but I'm optimistic."

"Vampires creep me out," Hudson said. "I can't imagine marrying one."

Bryn elbowed her brother. "First of all, that's rude. Second of all, you can't imagine marrying anybody, never mind a vampire."

"You'll have to excuse Hudson," Linnea said. "He gets his attitude about vampires from his father."

"Dad is plenty upset for Uncle Granger," Hudson said. "You should hear what he said about you."

Linnea shot him a threatening look. "Hudson. None of that bears repeating."

"I feel sorry for Uncle Granger, too," Bryn said, "but if Ember doesn't feel the same way about him, what's she supposed to do? Marry him out of pity?"

"There are worse reasons to marry," my aunt said.

I cast a surprised glance at her. "You never wanted me to marry Granger."

"No, but I'm not talking specifically about the sheriff. I simply mean that there are worse reasons to marry someone than pity."

"Such as?" Florian pressed.

"It doesn't matter," my aunt scoffed. "Where in Hecate's name is dinner?"

On cue, platters floated into the dining room and landed gently on the table. Ackley and Aspen cheered.

"They're hungry," Aster said apologetically. "They didn't get to eat after piano lessons."

"Those kids don't seem to have any down time," Florian said. "It's one scheduled activity after another."

Aster began serving food onto her sons' plates. "If they need any help with down time, at least they have the perfect uncle to assist them."

"Hey, that's uncalled for," Florian objected. "I've been doing well with the tourism board."

Aster handed the platter to her brother. "You're right. You have been. Maybe you can help Linnea out with marketing for Palmetto House."

"That's a wonderful idea," Aunt Hyacinth interjected.

"You just want to keep me busy and out of trouble," Florian said.

"And what's wrong with that?" my aunt replied. "I think it would be lovely to help your sister."

Linnea pushed the food around on her plate. "I really

could use the help. I feel like the inn is invisible lately. Maybe you could come up with one of your cute slogans like you did for Starry Hollow."

"You really want my help?" Florian seemed genuinely surprised.

"You'll come up with something awesome," Hudson said. "I don't care what my dad says, you're not a complete and total waste of space."

Linnea smacked her forehead. "Hudson, can you please insert a filter so that you don't repeat everything your father says? The world doesn't need that kind of energy."

Florian drank his ale. "No worries, Linnea. Wyatt's insults are pretty lame. Like him."

Linnea put a finger to her lips and glared at Florian. As much as Wyatt frustrated her, she didn't want anyone speaking poorly of him in front of his kids. I totally understood.

"Hey, why didn't you tell me you saw the sheriff patrolling the neighborhood?" I asked.

Florian stuck a forkful of sprouts in his mouth and chewed. "I didn't think it was a big deal. I mean, he's the sheriff and there was a murder so…"

"There was a murder?" Aspen asked.

"No, no, dear," Aster said. "Uncle Florian said there was a herd…of unicorns. They ran through the neighborhood the other day and Sheriff Nash was patrolling the area to make sure no one got hurt."

"Cool," Aspen said.

"How's the investigation going anyway?" Florian whispered.

I stared at my plate. "Kind of hitting a wall. We found evidence of a werewolf at the scene, but we're still identifying suspects."

"A werewolf, huh? Have you been to see Nola?" Florian asked.

"Who's Nola?" I asked.

"Hot werewolf. She lives over in the Pine Barrens," Florian said. "I knocked back a few pints with her at the Whitethorn recently. I thought I might…" His gaze flicked to Ackley and Aspen. "I thought I might make a new friend, but she wasn't interested. She was too busy stewing over Tatiana."

"You *saw* Tatiana?" I blurted.

"No, she'd already left," Florian said. "But Nola was still there. She seemed really distracted by the whole thing, like she'd spent the evening with a ghost and she couldn't handle it."

An upset werewolf was seen with the victim the night before her murder? "Thanks, Florian. That's really helpful." I made a mental note to text Deputy Bolan after dinner. The more suspects we interviewed, the sooner we'd catch Tatiana's killer.

I sailed into the office of *Vox Populi* the next morning and was immediately confronted by Bentley.

"Any updates on the investigation?" the elf asked.

I halted. "What's with the interest? Are you rooting for a certain outcome?"

"Alec wants me to start drafting the article, so I need your notes."

"Could you at least try not to look smug about it?" I asked.

Bentley smiled. "Nope."

"Why doesn't he want me to do it?" I asked.

"Why do you think?" the elf asked. "You're too close to it. He thinks I'll be unbiased."

"We're all close to it," I argued. "Alec was a suspect. Tanya…" I surveyed the room. "Where's Tanya?"

"She's running late," Bentley said. He held out his hand. "Your notes, please."

I swatted his hand away. "Since when does Tanya ever run late?" Our office manager ran a tight ship. That was the only option when Alec Hale was in charge.

"I think she's having a hard time," Bentley said. "She knows Tatiana wasn't the most beloved fairy in the world, but she was still Tanya's niece."

I brushed past him and went to my desk. "I get it, Bentley. Family is complicated. You don't need to convince me." I'd have to find a way to lift Tanya's spirits. Her feelings on the subject were no doubt complex and I could understand her wanting time alone to process.

"Should we send her a fruit basket?" Bentley asked.

I looked up at him. "With a note that says 'sorry about your murdered niece that everyone hated?'"

He rubbed his pointy ear. "Well, when you put it that way, my suggestion sounds stupid." He hesitated. "A box of chocolates?"

"I vote for a trip to the Whitethorn and getting her wasted when this is all over." I glanced back at the editor's office. "Is Alec here?"

"Don't you two keep tabs on each other now?" The elf returned to his desk and began typing away on the keyboard.

"Of course not." I pulled out my notes from the investigation and debated whether to hand them over. I decided to review them first. Sometimes reading the suspects' answers planted ideas that didn't occur to me at the time. I didn't realize Bentley was reading over my shoulder until he gasped.

"Wow! How many paranormals did Tatiana…? Forget it. By gumdrop, I hope Alec never sees this."

"Don't include it in the article and he won't," I said. "Make sure you pay attention to the parts I marked as confidential. Don't print those."

"I know how to do my job, Ember," he said testily. "I've been doing it for much longer than you, in case you've forgotten."

"How can I forget when you never let me?" I shot back.

The door opened and my heart stuttered as Alec entered the office, looking ridiculously handsome in a navy blue suit. The vampire never ceased to take my breath away. I wondered whether I would always feel this way about Alec. My smile gave my thoughts away because he came straight to my desk with a devilish glint in his eye.

"Miss Rose, you're looking particularly well today. The color of that top suits you."

Bentley adjusted his tie. "Ahem. Let's not cross over into any human resources violations."

Alec regarded him. "And that suit makes you look taller, Bentley."

The elf's back instantly straightened. "Thank you, sir. Meadow chose it for me."

"She has excellent taste," Alec said. "Miss Rose, I'd like to see you in about five minutes, if you would be so kind."

"Sure," I said. I watched Alec stride toward his office, enjoying the view.

"Just out of curiosity, does he call you Miss Rose in the bedroom too?" Bentley whispered.

"You'd better watch it," I said. "Vampire hearing." I tapped my ear.

"Let's not cross over into any human resources violations, shall we?" Alec called.

Bentley nearly keeled over. "Please don't ever break up with him. Old Alec would've drained my veins if he'd overheard a remark like that. New Alec is so much better."

I folded my arms. "Oh? So you're Team Alec now?"

"I've always been Team Alec," Bentley said. "He's been so much lighter this week. You heard him a minute ago. He complimented me. I don't think he's *ever* complimented me before."

I liked that I seemed to have a positive impact on Alec's mood. "Not to worry. I have no intention of breaking up with him." If anything, I worried about him breaking up with me. It was early days, though. I had to hope for the best.

Bentley seemed visibly relieved.

"How are the wedding plans coming along?" I asked. I was feeling benevolent toward the elf. He was still akin to the brother I never wanted, but even siblings experienced moments of peaceful co-existence.

"If you consider family squabbles progress, then it's going well," he confessed.

"Sorry to hear that. What's the issue?"

His eyebrows shot up. "You're interested?"

"Not really, but it'll kill five minutes before I go kiss my boyfriend in his office." Okay, peaceful co-existence was overrated.

Bentley shuddered at my comment. "There's drama with Meadow's uncle. He and his first wife are coming to the wedding, but his second wife is also invited because she was very involved in Meadow's upbringing. The wives are both angry that the other one is invited." He leaned his chin on the palm of his hand. "It's a mess."

"So wait. Her uncle is married to the second wife but attending with the first one?"

"No, he divorced the second wife to reunite with his first wife. They hated each other for years. Meadow said it was a bitter divorce, but apparently they rekindled their romance when he was separated from the second wife."

"I bet Meadow's feeling pretty confused right now."

"She's not used to her aunt and uncle getting along. For most of her childhood, they were at war and now—boom. They act like nothing bad ever happened between them and the second wife is on the outs."

My phone buzzed and an image of a cartoon bat with fangs flashed on my screen—my avatar for Alec. I smiled and pushed back my chair.

"Do I need to wear earplugs?" Bentley asked, crinkling his nose.

"Don't be ridiculous," I said and then smiled. "We'll be very quiet."

He made a horrified sound and I laughed as I hurried to Alec's office. I honestly had no idea why he needed to see me. It certainly wasn't to get horizontal since we'd agreed that wasn't an option at this stage.

"Hi," I said, closing the door behind me. "Everything okay?"

Alec smiled and his fangs peeked out from the corners of his mouth. "I suspect Bentley already asked for your notes."

"He basically tackled me when I came through the door." I made myself comfortable in the chair opposite him.

"Any progress on identifying the killer?" he asked.

"There was werewolf fur on Tatiana's wings," I said, "but they can't tie it to a specific werewolf. We've been collecting samples from the werewolves we interview."

Alec's expression shifted from curious to concerned. "Then you must have been able to rule out Sheriff Nash."

"Not yet," I said. "I got a text last night that the lab accidentally left the samples too close to an open flame and they disintegrated. Anyway, it's okay because there's another wolf on the list that we haven't spoken to yet, so we'll need her sample too," I said. "Her name is Nola. Deputy Bolan and I are going to speak to her shortly."

"A breakthrough, perhaps." He threaded his fingers together. "I apologize that this has fallen on your shoulders."

"Why should you apologize? It's not your fault."

"Still. It's a delicate situation under the circumstances. You've handled it impeccably, I might add. Not that I expected anything less from you. You've always impressed me, Ember. From the very first."

"The very first?" My body warmed all over. "Is this where we reminisce about the day we met?"

"Probably not the time or the place, though, I admit, I was drawn to you from the outset."

"You're not just saying all this to butter me up so I'll bump up my timeline?"

He wore a vague smile. "And which timeline would that be?"

"You know which timeline." I knocked on the desk for good measure.

"I wouldn't dream of trying to manipulate you in such a fashion," he said. "Regardless, when our physical union finally takes place, it will not be in an office."

I cocked an eyebrow. "No?"

"Certainly not. It might surprise you to learn that I've imagined the moment many times."

I tried to appear casual though my pulse was racing. "Nope. Doesn't surprise me. I'm very imaginable."

He chuckled.

My phone buzzed and I recognized the refrain from *Come On Eileen*—the ringtone I set for Deputy Bolan. "Looks like my other timeline has been bumped up. I need to go."

Disappointment rippled across his handsome features. "So soon? I was rather enjoying our chat."

"There are plenty of chats in our future, Alec," I said, heading for the door. "That's the beauty of being in a relationship."

CHAPTER FOURTEEN

Nola Burrows lived in an isolated part of the Pine Barrens. Most shifter communities in Starry Hollow were tight-knit, but Nola seemed to have distanced herself from the pack. Her rustic log cabin was obscured by a protective circle of trees. The front yard was decorated with metal sculptures in a variety of shapes. I noted flowers, the sun, and the phases of the moon.

Deputy Bolan headed straight for the front door. I hung back, feeling a stir in the air around us.

"She isn't inside," I said. I wasn't sure how I knew, but I did.

The leprechaun turned around to look at me. "You're psychic now?"

"Hey, I meet with Marigold every week," I said. "Maybe it's finally rubbing off on me." The Mistress-of-Psychic Skills would be pleased to know her time with me wasn't in vain.

A low growl made the hair on my arms stand on end. Slowly, I twisted to glimpse the source. A white wolf stood behind me, teeth bared. I held up my hands, the international sign for 'don't shoot,' or in this case—'don't give me a fatal werewolf bite.'

"Nola?" I said calmly.

The wolf snapped her powerful jaws.

"Rose, you should take a step back toward me," Deputy Bolan advised softly.

"No," I said. "That's closer to her house. She'll feel threatened."

"I feel threatened right now and so should you," the leprechaun pointed out.

I kept my focus on the wolf. "My name is Ember Rose." I adopted my most soothing tone—the one I used when trying to encourage PP3 to swallow his flea and tick pills. "Deputy Bolan and I would like to speak with you regarding an important matter. We need your help."

The wolf ceased snarling but didn't take human form.

"Maybe I should show her my badge," the deputy said. He moved to unpin it from his shirt and the wolf took a menacing step forward. "Or maybe not."

"We need to talk to you about a fairy called Tatiana," I said. "I think you know her."

The wolf howled. The sound was angry and haunting. Why didn't she shift?

"Nola, we can't speak to you like this," I said. "We need you in human form." Despite my calm appearance, my insides were quivering. If Nola was responsible for killing Tatiana, she might have no problem adding the deputy and I to the body count.

"If she won't cooperate, we'll have to bring her in to the office," the leprechaun said. "How many pounds of unconscious werewolf can you lift?"

The wolf growled and I glanced at the deputy. "Permission to encourage her cooperation here, Deputy?" I wasn't keen on transporting Nola anywhere in her wolf form.

"Permission granted."

I pulled out my wand and took aim. "Last chance to cooperate, Nola." A single leap and her jaws could easily clamp down on my throat.

The wolf's amber eyes narrowed at the sight of my wand. Still, she made no move to shift. I hated to follow through on my plan, but it was better than resorting to violence. I summoned my magic and flicked the wand at one of the metal sculptures. "*Fuego!*" The sun caught fire.

The wolf whimpered.

I aimed my wand at the next sculpture. "I'll destroy them all if you don't shift right now." I kept my voice firm even though I remained petrified inside.

Nola finally shifted. "Put out that fire!" she yelled. "Do you have any idea how long it took me to get the rays exactly right on that sun?"

I pointed my wand and said, "*Dissipo.*" The fire went out, leaving no visible damage to the sculpture.

Nola's human form was almost as pale as her wolf form. Her strawberry blond hair was shoulder-length and wild. She made no move to preserve her modesty. Instead, she sauntered up to the front door and opened it. "I suppose you'll want a cup of tea or something. Sorry, I only have ale or hard alcohol."

"Nothing for me," Deputy Bolan said.

"That's because you only like umbrella drinks," I said.

He shot me an innocent look. "What's not to like?"

We followed the werewolf inside and I closed the door behind us. The interior of the cabin was basically the same as the exterior, except for the addition of furniture and appliances. There was no decor. No framed photos or artwork on the walls. Nothing of a personal nature. The only items that seemed to reflect Nola were the metal sculptures in the garden.

Nola grabbed a short robe from a nearby hook and headed straight to the modest kitchen. She pulled a bottle off the shelf. "I think I know why you're here." She produced two pint glasses and a shot glass. "Moonshine, ale, or burstberry vodka? I made the moonshine myself."

"Ale for me," I said.

She popped the lid off a bottle with her teeth and poured the ale. It was an interesting shade of purple and I couldn't imagine which type of ale produced such a color. It occurred to me that Sheriff Nash would know, which immediately resulted in guilt forming a tight ball in my stomach.

"So why do you think we're here?" I asked, as I brought the glass of ale to my lips and sniffed. There was a vague fruity scent to it.

"Tatiana is back in Starry Hollow and she's no doubt swindled some poor soul out of his prized possession. Let me guess." She snapped her fingers. "A classic car."

"Not quite," I said. "How did you know she was here?" I took a hesitant sip of the ale. Not too bad.

"I picked up her scent early this week, when I went for a midnight run," Nola said. "At first I thought I'd imagined it. That it was only a flash of memory." A wistful look passed over her features.

"How did you figure out it was more than a memory?" the deputy asked.

"I saw her," Nola said simply. "The next day." She poured burstberry vodka into the shot glass and downed it in one swift move.

"Where?" the deputy asked.

"She was in the Whitethorn," Nola said.

"You just happened to run into her?" I asked.

"No, I tracked her there," Nola admitted. "Once I had her scent, I couldn't let it go."

Hmm. "Was she surprised to see you?" I asked.

Nola opened the moonshine and poured herself a glass. "If she was, she didn't show it. Tatiana was always good at maintaining a blank face when she needed to. One of her many talents."

"Did the two of you talk?" Deputy Bolan asked.

"Yes, over a few drinks. Did a bit of catching up." She pressed her lips together. "Same old Tatiana."

"In what way?" I asked.

She took a thoughtful sip of moonshine. "New town. No job. New guys, always plural, that one. Somehow still looked like a million bucks. The usual."

"How was your conversation with her?" I asked. "Upbeat? No arguments?"

"Tatiana is always a good time," Nola said. "I think she had everyone in the bar wrapped around her pinky finger before she left. Even that smutty parrot adores her."

"Maybe not everyone," I said. "Someone was definitely unhappy with Tatiana."

Nola leaned her hip against the counter. "What makes you say that?"

"Because someone killed her," the deputy said. "She's dead."

Nola's hand froze partway to her mouth. "Dead?"

"Drowned," I said. "In her aunt's swimming pool. Not an accident."

Nola gulped the rest of her drink and continued to grip the empty glass in her hand. "That can't be true. Tatiana is... She's a force of nature." Nola blinked away tears. "She's not capable of dying unless she wants to be dead."

"She was mortal and vulnerable to all the same dangers as most of us," I said. "And someone made sure that she died in that pool."

Nola squeezed her eyes closed for a brief moment before

opening them again. "Do you have any leads? Is that the reason you're here?"

"We found wolf fur at the crime scene," I said. I didn't mention where. I wanted to see if she knew more than she was saying.

Nola's expression remained neutral. "Tatiana pissed off more than a few werewolves when she lived here, probably even more than I'm aware of." She inhaled deeply. "And I guess the fact that I'm a wolf means I'm a suspect."

"We understand you were friends before she moved away," I said. "We were wondering if you'd kept in touch."

"No, that wasn't her style," Nola said. "She burned every bridge and kept on driving."

"Would you mind if we take a look around?" Deputy Bolan asked.

Nola laughed. "To find what? A soggy towel to prove I drowned her? Sure. Have at it." She waved a hand. "Knock yourselves out. I don't have much." She swayed slightly as she refilled her glass. If she kept up the pace, she'd be passed out within the hour.

The deputy and I went from room to room, although I wasn't sure what I was searching for. A journal with all her misdeeds? A list of naughty friends with Tatiana's name crossed out?

Deputy Bolan seemed to read my mind. "Sometimes you don't know what you're looking for until you see it," he said.

It was in her bedroom that I found it. "Would you mind coming in here, Nola?" I called.

"What is it?" Deputy Bolan asked. I gestured to the ceiling.

Nola appeared in the doorway. "You found a murder weapon? Because I doubt a swimming pool fits in here." Her laugh was awkward and high-pitched. Drunk laughter.

I pointed to the metal sculpture that hung from the ceiling above the bed. It was larger than any of the others in the garden, with wings spread wide and covered in a sheen of bronze glitter.

A fairy.

"When did you make this?" I asked, fixated on the sculpture. It had been masterfully crafted with details that were lacking in any of the other sculptures.

"Two years ago when I was between jobs," Nola said. "Took longer than usual, but the results are worth it."

"Why not display it outside with the rest of them?" Deputy Bolan said.

Nola's cheeks grew flushed. "This wasn't made to go in my garden."

"Why not?" the deputy asked. "It's the best one I've seen."

"I think she was only going for artistic expression," I said, studying the sculpture. "It radiates warmth and light."

Deputy Bolan rolled his eyes. "There you go with your psychic babble again."

"It's *psycho* babble," I corrected him.

He snickered. "I'll say."

I ignored him and returned my focus to the fairy sculpture. There was something about its placement, too, that suggested a favored status. It wasn't that Nola didn't find it good enough to display in the garden. It was more that she didn't want to. This sculpture was for her eyes only. She prayed to it every night before she went to sleep, as though it were a wishing star. And I knew exactly what she wished for.

"You were in love with her," I said quietly.

Nola averted her gaze from the sculpture. "Who?"

I gave her a pointed look. "You know who."

Deputy Bolan's small head whipped toward the werewolf. "You had a thing for Tatiana?"

Nola glowered at him. "Is that really so hard to believe in this day and age, Deputy?"

"No," the deputy replied. "And I would know. So would my husband, for that matter."

Nola's mouth opened and closed. "I see," she finally said. "I'm sure it's different for leprechauns."

Deputy Bolan eyed her. "Different how?"

"Shifters, werewolves in particular, have a certain mentality," Nola explained. "The pack is very traditional. Alpha, beta. Pups for the propagation of the species."

"I dated a werewolf," I said. "He seemed perfectly willing to marry a witch." Sheriff Nash hadn't been the least bit concerned with pack mentality. Neither had Wyatt Nash when he married Linnea.

Nola sighed in exasperation. "We're Arctic wolves. We're endangered. The last thing anyone in my pack wants is for a wolf of childbearing age to follow any other path except for the one that involves mating with another Arctic werewolf and having little Arctic pups."

"Yet here you are years later with no mate and no pups," the deputy said.

"And why do you think I live among them and yet apart?" she shot back. "They don't want to shun me. They keep hoping I come back to the fold and do my duty." She lifted her chin a fraction. "I'm not about to sacrifice myself for the sake of the pack."

"Not exactly pack mentality, is it?" I asked.

Her amber eyes shone with pain. "If you'd been treated the way I have, you would understand why I don't care."

Deputy Bolan moved to stand in front of her. "I do understand, Nola. Believe me, I do." He reached to comfort her and it would have been a lovely moment, except for the fact that he couldn't reach her shoulder. Then it became awkward when his hand landed on her boob. She stared at the offending extremity until he removed it, red-faced.

"Maybe we should leave my bedroom now," Nola slurred.

The three of us returned to the kitchen where Nola took possession of her glass once again. I fought the urge to remove it from her grasp. This was her home and it wasn't my place.

"Did you ever tell Tatiana how you felt?" I asked.

"Of course," Nola said. "I'm not shy. I was drawn to her immediately. I mean, I waited until I had a sense of her first, so that I wasn't coming out of nowhere with it."

"What made you decide it was safe to tell her?" Deputy Bolan asked. "I remember what dating was like before my husband. I felt like I was blind and drunk on a regular basis."

"That about sums it up," Nola said. "Tatiana made it easy, though. Or so I believed. One night after a drunken escapade involving a unicorn and a ball of yarn, she kissed me."

I wasn't even going to touch the part about the unicorn and the ball of yarn. "*She* kissed you?"

Nola nodded and her eyes swelled with tears. "I thought this was it. I'd found my soulmate. That she was someone like me, unafraid to live an authentic life. The next night I invited her to dinner and I told her I wanted a relationship with her."

"And then what happened?" Deputy Bolan asked.

Nola stared blankly at the far wall. "She laughed."

My heart seized. "She laughed?"

Nola managed a small smile. "Humiliating, right? She told me it was all in good fun, that she was drunk and would've made out with a lamp post had one been near enough. She told me I didn't appeal to her."

It sounded as though Tatiana didn't mince words. "That must've been very painful for you."

Nola slammed down another shot and smacked her lips together, seeming to enjoy the burn in her throat. "Worst day of my life."

"How did you react?" I asked.

She shrugged. "My usual defensive mechanism. I got angry. Pushed over the table and screamed obscenities at her. She sat there and smiled the whole time. She seemed to enjoy my outrage." Nola winced at the memory. "I made a fool of myself and she lapped up every second of it."

"Tatiana sounds like a sociopath," I said.

Nola was silent for a moment. "I would have loved her anyway."

"Would she have been worth it, though?" I asked. "She would've hurt you over and over again. Consider it a blessing that she left town." And that she was dead.

"She wouldn't have been happy with anyone," Nola admitted. "She was too selfish and burned through relationships quickly. I bet that centaur she left town with only last a few months at the most."

"You didn't ask her about it when you saw her at the bar?" I asked.

"No," Nola said. "She mentioned a few guys' names, but I didn't ask for details. I was only interested in her."

"How did it feel to see her again?" I asked.

"Honestly? Exhilarating," she replied.

"It didn't stir up old wounds or anger?" I asked.

"The anger faded a long time ago," Nola said. "Tatiana couldn't help being irresistible."

"No, but she could help being a horrible creature," Deputy Bolan said.

"She was in a fine mood when I saw her," Nola said. "She even brought up the night she kissed me. Didn't seem to remember laughing at me the next day though. She only reminisced about the fun parts. It made me miss her like crazy." Nola hugged herself. "Brought all those feelings back to the surface, even though I knew she hadn't changed her mind about me."

It wasn't her mind that would've needed to change. It was her entire being.

"Why do you think she spent time with you if she wasn't interested?" I asked.

Nola poured herself another drink. "What do you mean?"

"She usually had a motive for getting involved with someone," I said. "Money, power, access. What was her reason for bringing you into her orbit?"

She tapped her short, sensible fingernails on the side of her glass. "Amusement, if I had to guess. I kept her entertained."

"And power," Deputy Bolan said. "She was smart. She probably sensed how you felt about her from the start and thought it would be fun to see how far she could push you."

Nola's expression hardened. "I never said she was nice."

"No," I agreed. "I don't think anyone has said that to describe Tatiana."

"Did she leave the Whitethorn with anyone the other night?" I asked.

Nola shook her head. "I watched her go. She said she was meeting someone to claim her inheritance the next day. That they were bringing it to her aunt's house."

"Did she say who left the inheritance or what it was?" Deputy Bolan asked.

"She didn't know," Nola said. "She said it was a big mystery and she couldn't wait to find out. She only planned to stay in town long enough to collect and then she was hightailing out of here again."

The fact that the inheritance was still a mystery bothered me. It had to be connected to her death.

"Just for the record," the deputy said, "where were you on Monday between the hours of nine and three?"

Nola stared into her glass. "A couple of those hours, I was at a pack meeting."

"In daylight?" the deputy asked. "Isn't that unusual?"

"Our alpha is unwell," she said. "It was an emergency meeting to discuss a new beta, should the need arise."

That would be easy enough to verify. "I hope Ferdinand is okay," Deputy Bolan said.

"I'll be sure to give him your well wishes."

"We'd also like a patch of your fur," I said. "To see if it matches the one on file. Just standard procedure."

Nola's mouth formed a thin line. "It won't."

"Even so, we need to log it into evidence," the deputy said.

"Evidence that isn't left next to an open flame this time," I said archly.

"Fine. It's easy enough to dust off the floor. The stuff gets everywhere." Nola brought the drink to her lips and paused. "It seems strange that someone would have left her anything. I've been imagining that it's a steaming pile of garbage, that they lured her here to screw with her. It's the kind of stunt she would've pulled."

"We've been trying to figure out who might have had a soft spot for her," the deputy said.

Nola's lips formed a half smile. "Besides me? I think I'm the only one who was stupid enough to hold out hope for her."

"Even if she were still alive, I wouldn't have recommended it," I said. Tatiana would never have changed, not for anyone or anything.

Nola set down the glass, unable to finish it. "Maybe this is just the news I needed to hear."

"To cheer up?" the deputy asked.

Nola unclenched her fingers from the glass. "To let go."

CHAPTER FIFTEEN

"I can't believe this party is for me," Marley said, as we entered the grand foyer of Thornhold. There were so many cars parked outside that I wondered whether everyone in town had ended up invited.

"Aunt Hyacinth has been hoping you'd be one of us," I said. "It's her subtle and wealthy way of saying 'hooray.'"

Aunt Hyacinth's right hand intercepted us in the foyer. "Welcome, Miss Ember," Simon said. "Miss Marley."

I was about to compliment his shiny shoes when I noticed the decorations. "This house looks amazing," I said. The interior had been transformed into a magical wonderland. Tiny fey lights glittered all around us. It was as though we'd entered a forest.

"Is the whole house like this?" Marley asked. Her blue eyes had never been bigger.

"It is, miss," Simon told her. "You should see the ballroom. That's where most of the guests have congregated."

"Seriously?" I asked. Aunt Hyacinth rarely opened the ballroom for events. Apparently, it had once been a regular feature of Thornhold parties, but that was back when her husband was still alive.

Marley's voice dropped to a whisper. "Why would she go to so much trouble for me?"

I pulled her close and kissed her forehead. "Nothing is too much trouble for you. You're a special girl, Marley Rose, and don't you ever forget it."

"I'm a special *witch*," Marley said proudly.

"That too," I agreed. We left Simon at his post by the door and made our way to the ballroom. We passed a bubbling cauldron that filled the house with a wonderful aroma of spices. Tree branches arched at the ceiling and I inhaled the smell of sandalwood as we continued to the ballroom. Soft music played in the distance and Marley gripped my hand and squeezed.

"I'm a witch, Mom," she said. "I have magic powers."

I smiled. "I know. Pretty cool, right?"

She shivered with excitement. "The coolest. I wish my classmates in New Jersey could see me now."

"You could change your Facebook profile to 'witch.'"

Marley rolled her eyes. "Facebook is for old people, Mom."

As we crossed the threshold into the ballroom, the room exploded with applause. Marley beamed with pride as familiar faces congratulated her. I took a step to the side to grant her the spotlight and surveyed the ballroom. A faux full moon shone overhead. It looked authentic thanks to my aunt's magic. An ice sculpture dominated the middle of the dance floor. It was carved into a likeness of the witch statue mounted on the top of coven headquarters. Like the statue, the sculpture held a flat disc over her head to signify the silver moon of our coven. It rested in an empty round pool, presumably to catch any drippings.

I glimpsed the headdress of the High Priestess over by the

snack table. Iris Sandstone's willowy frame lingered by the crudités. She was deep in conversation with Wren and I fought the urge to grill the Master-of-Incantation about his budding romance with Delphine.

A cool hand rested on my shoulder. "Even from the back, you are a vision."

I whirled around to see Alec gazing at me with an intensity that triggered every nerve ending in my body. I pressed my hands against his firm chest. "Hello, handsome. When did you get here?"

He leaned down and kissed me. "Only half an hour ago," he said. "Hyacinth has spared no expense, I see."

"Are you surprised? She won't be doing this again until Ackley and Aspen come of age," I said. The four-year-old twins had a while to go yet.

He slipped an arm around my waist. "It feels like the entire town is here."

"That was my thought, too." I wasn't sure what the ballroom's capacity was, but my aunt was definitely aiming to meet it with this crowd. "Maybe I should do more digging about Tatiana. If everyone is here, then someone here must know *something*."

Alec cast me a sidelong glance. "A dead end with the she-wolf?"

"Most likely," I replied. "We sent her fur sample to the lab to see if it matches. No word yet, though." I spotted the sheriff chatting with two members of the Council of Elders by the ice sculpture. "I should say hello to Sheriff Nash."

Alec squeezed my shoulder. "I assume it's best that I don't cross paths with him."

"Not here," I agreed. "I'll be back in a minute." I maneuvered my way through the throng of bodies to the ice sculpture.

"And here's the lucky mother now." Misty Brookline flapped her yellow fairy wings.

"Congratulations, Ember," Arthur Rutledge said. The elder werewolf greeted me with a warm smile. "You must be very proud."

"Well, I can't take credit for genetics," I said. "They have a will all their own."

Arthur chuckled. "The sheriff tells me you're on the hunt for a werewolf. Do let me know if I can be of assistance. I may not be an alpha, but as an Elder, I have a certain degree of influence."

"The fairies are also very keen to help," Misty said. "Tatiana may have not been a model member of the community, but she was one of ours all the same."

"Thank you," I said. "Deputy Bolan and I have been following up every available lead, but I'll let you know if we need anything from you."

"I gave my second fur sample to the lab, so hopefully I can join the investigation as soon as I'm cleared," the sheriff said.

"Too bad the lab is closed on weekends," Misty said. "It would be good to have you back at the helm." She smiled at me. "Not that we don't appreciate your efforts, dear."

Arthur clapped Sheriff Nash on the back. "Another ale, Granger? Yours is dangerously low."

The sheriff gave a gruff nod. "That'd be great, Arthur."

"I'll join you," Misty said. "Standing this close to the ice sculpture is making me chilly."

I waited a beat for them to leave before facing the sheriff. "It's nice of you to be here," I said. "I'm sure you'd rather be anywhere else right now."

Sheriff Nash swigged the remainder of his ale. "I'm happy to be here for Marley, Rose. She's a great kid and she'll be a talented witch, just like her mom."

My heart swelled. "I'm glad you feel that way."

"Of course. Why wouldn't I?" His expression soured. "Do you really think I'd let my disappointment in us affect my opinion of your daughter? That's not the kind of man I am, Rose. I think you know me better than that."

He was right. I did. I remembered the locket he'd given Marley for her birthday, the one that displayed a photo of me on one side and of her father on the other. It had been a thoughtful gift and I loved him for it.

But not enough.

Arthur returned with the sheriff's ale and I politely excused myself. The sheriff had probably endured as much of me today as he could handle. I didn't want to push it.

I turned around and walked straight into the massive chest of Zale Murphy, the merman who saved Aunt Hyacinth from drowning in the ocean.

"Sorry about that." I tipped my chin up to look at him. "How are you, Zale?"

"Pleased to be invited," he replied. "Your aunt seemed hesitant to include me at first, but she came around."

"She's not someone who's quick to welcome change," I said. "I'm impressed you've made it this far already."

He offered a slight bow. "Hyacinth is a jewel to be treasured. I have the patience of the sea at my disposal."

"Good, because you'll need it."

The ring of Aunt Hyacinth's bell quieted everyone. The music came to a halt and the guests craned their necks to pinpoint the location of the hostess. In true diva form, my aunt levitated above the crowd in a golden kaftan and matching heels in order to address them. She held Precious in her arms and I laughed at the sight of the cat's golden circlet.

"Greetings Silver Moon witches and wizards and esteemed guests," she began. "As you know, we are here today to celebrate as we welcome my lovely great-niece, Marley, into the bosom of our beloved coven."

I hope she doesn't mean her actual bosom. Raoul's voice filled my head. *She could suffocate the entire coven with those weapons of mass destruction.*

Raoul? I hissed. I looked around but couldn't see him in the crowd.

What? he replied. *She can't hear me.*

But I can and it's distracting. What are you doing here?

What am I ever doing anywhere? he said. *There's food.*

You need to go, I said. *There's enough going on without you in the mix.*

Are your two boyfriends giving you trouble?

I do not have two boyfriends. I have one and he's coming toward me now with a flute of bucksberry fizz.

The other one looks angsty. Maybe get him a flute of fizz before he starts issuing tickets to the parked cars.

Go. Away. I returned my focus to my aunt's speech.

"We expect incredible things from this young witch. She is, after all, a descendant of the One True Witch. I look forward to seeing her perform wonderful magic for years to come."

There was a smattering of applause.

Alec nuzzled my ear as he handed me the flute. "And I look forward to having you perform your magic on me for years to come."

"Works both ways," I said softly.

His expression smoldered. "So it does."

"Marley, I believe you've been preparing a small presentation of your magic," my aunt said.

I stiffened. Marley had been preparing a magical presentation? When? I watched as my aunt conjured a spell to bring Marley level with her in the air. My daughter seemed perfectly at ease, as though she'd levitated a hundred times already.

"What in sweet Elvis's name?" I said in a hushed tone.

"What's the matter?" Alec asked.

I observed my daughter as she held her wand, completely poised, and aimed it at the ceiling. She said a word in Latin that I completely missed because I was too busy wondering when she had time to practice magic behind my back. Fireworks erupted over our heads with colorful sparks shooting in all directions. The guests ooh-ed and aah-ed and then clapped wildly.

"Marley's doing real magic," I said.

Alec chuckled. "What did you expect?"

I stared at my daughter in awe. "She looks so beautiful up there. So grown up." It hit me how quickly time was passing. She was already eleven. Eleven! When did that happen? Most of the time when I looked at her, I still saw the scared little girl who insisted on sleeping with the lights on.

"You've done an amazing job with her," Alec said. "You should be proud."

Marley and Aunt Hyacinth returned to the floor and the music resumed. Linnea waved to me from across the room. Nope, not waved. Gestured. I followed the motion of her hand and saw Wyatt ambling toward us. Oh, I understood. Linnea was warning me.

"If it isn't the lovely couple." Wyatt Nash shuffled in front of us, grinning. "What does it matter whose heart you break as long as you're happy, am I right?"

"That's rich coming from you," I said.

"Someone's taken a swim in the punch bowl, I smell," Alec said. "Tell me, Wyatt, did you manage to leave any for the rest of us?"

Wyatt pushed his finger into Alec's chest. "You don't

belong here. You're not family." His pronunciation of 'family' was barely intelligible.

"Technically, you're not family either," I said.

Wyatt pursed his lips. "Ooh, fighting words from the heartbreaker. Maybe it should have been you in that pool instead of Tatiana."

Alec's fangs slipped out and he stared at Wyatt with an intensity that put me on edge. I couldn't let this escalate, not here in the grand ballroom of Thornhold. My aunt would never forgive me.

I placed myself between them and pulled out my wand. "Not another move. I have a wand and I'm not afraid to use it."

"Hey," Wyatt slurred. "That's my line."

I ignored him. "Alec, please. Stand down."

One glance at me and the vampire retracted his fangs. "Would you like to dance, Ember?" Alec asked.

"A dance sounds perfect." I said. Anything to put distance between Wyatt and us.

Alec took my hand and we started for the dance floor. As we passed the ice sculpture, Alec released my hand and whirled around. Wyatt was mid-air, having launched himself at the vampire. They collided and smashed into the ice sculpture. The witch cracked in half and both pieces fell into the empty pool.

"You've got to be kidding me," I heard Linnea exclaim. She crossed the room at warp speed. "Wyatt Nash, you get out of there right now! You're embarrassing your kids."

Wyatt had already shifted into his wolf form and he and Alec tousled in the empty pool next to the fallen sculpture.

Sheriff Nash appeared beside me. "What happened?"

"Your brother happened," I said. The sheriff started forward and I quickly blocked him. "Please don't."

"This is my fault, Rose," he said. "I need to get it under control."

"Not by joining in," I said.

Alec's fangs were on full display as he pinned the wolf down. A crowd had gathered around the pool. Linnea extended her wand and sparks streaked from the tip. They missed Wyatt and hit the halves of the sculpture, melting the ice. Water filled the pool as the two men continued their fight, oblivious to their environment. Alec's neatly pressed shirt was now torn, exposing his powerful muscles. Water splashed across the floor and both men became completely submerged.

I reached for my wand just as a body flew past me. Zale Murphy's fins slapped the top of the water before disappearing. The merman rose out of the water a moment later, holding a naked Wyatt by the scruff of his human neck. Alec crawled over the side of the pool, still clothed but soaking wet. Both men were bloody and bruised.

Alec staggered over to me and I wrapped my arms around him.

The sheriff scratched the back of his head. "Sorry about that, Hale. My brother gets carried away sometimes."

"It isn't your fault," Alec said stiffly.

The sheriff nodded and went to intercept his brother as Zale set Wyatt on the floor. Linnea conjured a clothing spell to take care of her ex-husband's nudity problem.

"Mom, is everything okay?" Marley drew alongside me, a worried expression on her face.

"I'm sorry, honey," I said. "Things got out of hand, but they're fine now."

"My sincerest apologies for ruining your party," Alec said.

Marley faced him. "Are you kidding? Everyone will be talking about this for ages. It's awesome!" She skipped away merrily and I felt my body relax.

"I doubt your aunt will be so forgiving," Alec said. "Perhaps I should speak with her now."

"No, you should see if there's a healer around." In this busy room, there had to be more than a few.

Alec kissed my forehead. "I'm a vampire, Ember. I'll heal quite quickly without assistance."

"Let me at least do a spell to fix your shirt."

He clasped my hand. "Somewhere away from prying eyes, please."

I guided him out of the ballroom and down the hall to my aunt's office.

"This won't hurt a bit," I teased. I gathered my will to me and aimed my wand. "*Emendo.*"

Alec glanced down at his mended clothes. "I do apologize if I embarrassed you. Fighting isn't typical for me."

"I know." I sidled up to him. "And not that I condone fighting, but watching you…" I sucked in a breath. "I don't know if it's the contrast between the suit and the alpha male or what."

The vampire's mouth quirked. "What don't you know?"

I shook my head, trying to get a grip. Now wasn't the time to turn to jelly. "Nothing. We should go."

Alec edged closer. "Any particular place in mind?"

Great balls of hotness. I could think of a dozen places I'd like to go with him right now. "The cottage is close," I squeaked. My hand flew to cover my mouth. I'd intended to sound normal, not like a deranged chipmunk.

His lips parted, revealing his impressive fangs and my knees weakened. "Are you certain?"

I stared up at him, my heart pounding. "No."

Alec closed the small gap between us and his lips found mine. "Come home with me," he murmured.

"Can't," I rasped. "We're not ready."

"Move forward another inch," he said, "and I think you'll find that I am."

Heat rose to my cheeks. "You know what I mean."

His mouth moved to my neck and my whole body vibrated with need. When the tip of his fangs escaped my bare skin, a moan escaped me.

"We're two consenting adults," he said, before gently nipping my earlobe. I felt ready to explode.

"Two adults who consented to build a solid foundation first," I replied. My eyes remained closed as he continued to explore me.

"I'll find the next counselor, if you'll permit me," he said.

I wanted to permit him anything he wanted right now, but I knew I couldn't. "Yes," I said.

"Yes to everything?"

I pulled away and smiled. "No." I noticed that his wounds were almost healed. "You weren't kidding about not needing a healer."

Alec fixed his collar. "It isn't often that I engage in brutality. Only when provoked." His eyes glinted with mischief. "Though now that I know how much it appeals to you…"

I grabbed him by the hand. "Let's go back to the ballroom. You owe me a dance."

He bowed. "As you wish."

I refused to budge, no matter how much I wanted more with him. There would be time. Alec Hale was immortal, after all. He had all the time in the world.

CHAPTER SIXTEEN

We parked a reasonable distance from the dump entrance. I didn't want to tip off Mr. Big Shot Crow that Raoul was arriving with a magical entourage. It might give him time to mobilize his own crew, or whatever thug crows did.

We filed in through the gap in the barbed wire fence.

"Be careful, Marley," I said.

She made a surprised face. "I'm so glad you said that because I was just about to rub my face on this sharp piece of fence."

"No need to go full teen on me," I said. "You've still got a couple of years." I glared at her before turning back around.

There he is, Raoul said. *In the recent rubbish section.*

The crow was using his beak to poke through a pile of garbage. His feathers were matted and one leg appeared lightly chewed. He wore a red rubber band around the other leg, just as Raoul had described. He looked unhealthy. I felt a pang of sympathy, until he turned and saw us. His beady eyes narrowed.

Go ahead, Raoul, I urged. *You're up.*

His dark eyes grew round and worried. *Throw me to the wolves, why don't you?*

He's a crow, I said.

Marley must have sensed his hesitation. "We've got this," she whispered. "Now show that crow who's king of the heap."

Raoul scampered over to the garbage heap and began to rummage. When he saw an item he wanted, he reached for it. The crow lunged and forced him back. Chills traveled down my spine, but I knew it wasn't my fear.

It was my familiar's.

Raoul made a hissing noise at the crow and the large black bird attacked. He flew at the raccoon and used his beak as a weapon, stabbing Raoul's body.

"Mom, do something!" Marley pleaded.

I produced my wand and aimed it at the trash surrounding the crow. I focused my will and commanded, "*Surgo.*"

Every piece of garbage shot into the air and swirled around the crow on all sides. He tried to fly upward and escape the trash prison, but I quickly moved more trash around him. He flapped his dark wings, unsure what to do next.

Drop a microwave on his head, Raoul said.

I'm not trying to kill him, I argued. *I just want to give him a taste of his own medicine.*

The crow was none too pleased with this turn of events. When he realized his goal of escaping the garbage was fruitless, he turned his attention to me. He cawed loudly and animals scampered out of their hiding places. Despite Raoul's fear coursing through my veins, I wasn't afraid. I was fortunate that I'd never been afraid of bullies. My father had taught me early on how to handle myself. My first experience was with a mean girl when I was in fourth grade. She'd tried to bully me on the playground. Ignoring her didn't do the trick so I'd complained to my dad. He told me to stand up to her and show her that I wasn't afraid. When she tried to force me off the swing I was on, I dug in and refused to move. No matter how hard she pushed me, I stayed on that swing. In fact, I stayed on that swing until recess was over and my teacher came to urge me to come inside. I got in trouble for ignoring the bell, but it worked like a charm. The girl never bothered me again.

The crow launched himself forward, a dangerous gleam in his eyes. He burst through the trash and landed on a pile of electronics nearby. The crow looked ready to rumble.

I aimed my wand. "You do not want to take another step, friend," I warned. "There's a lot more magic where that came from."

The crow inched forward, testing me. The crowd of animals gathered behind him to observe the standoff.

"I am not here to hurt you," I continued, "but I'll tell you right now, you'd better leave my familiar alone from now on or you're going to end up without any feathers."

The crow launched himself at me, screeching.

"*Affigo!*" Magic streaked from my wand and a cloud of trash surrounded the crow again, before getting sucked to him like a magnet. The weight of the trash dragged him to the ground. The crow stood and shook off the pile. Debris covered every inch of his feathers and curly pink ribbons dangled from his left wing. The crowd of animals tittered— laughter from the peanut gallery.

The crow shook off the accessories. His gaze darted to Raoul and I knew he was going to attack. Marley must have sensed it, too, because we both threw ourselves between the bird and the raccoon at the same time. Even Bonkers got in the act, swooping from on high and swatting the crow's head with an adorable wing.

The crow glanced back at the coterie of animals as though to see whether they planned to help him. No one moved. He jerked his head back to confront the two wands aimed at him.

"This is a huge dump," Marley said. "There's no reason why you can't share what's here."

And I was here first, Raoul said, stomping his paw for good measure.

Not helping, I told him over my shoulder.

The crow regarded us with tired eyes. He seemed beaten down, as though the mere thought of another confrontation was more than he could handle. Whatever fire he'd had in his belly was gone.

I lowered my wand and Marley followed suit. "Listen," I began, "my daughter is right. This place has plenty of trash for anyone that wants it. There's no need to be territorial."

"And you each have skills that could help the other," Marley pointed out. "Raoul is really good at finding the most valuable items. You're a crow. I bet you're good at reaching trash that no one else can."

"You could accomplish so much more together than at odds with each other," I added. I sounded like an after school special, but it seemed to work.

Raoul peered at the crow from around my legs. *Truce?*

The crow cawed. I couldn't understand him, but my familiar seemed to.

You can go now, Raoul said. *I've got it covered from here.*

"I'm going to need a shower when I get home," I said. "I reek."

What else is new? My familiar said and wisely hurried out of reach.

Marley looped her arm through mine. "Our work here is done."

. . .

166

No matter how many times I visited the Whitethorn, I never stopped expecting to see a hobbit holding a pint too big for his tiny hand. With its thatched roof and arched wooden door, the white building would have looked perfectly at home in Middle Earth.

I stepped up to the bar to wait for Alec. We agreed to meet for a drink at the pub and review a couple of counselors Alec found.

Captain Yellowjacket smiled, revealing his stained teeth. "Ember, it's good to see you." He lowered his voice. "I heard about you and the sheriff. If I'm being honest, I was sorry to hear the news."

"Thanks, it wasn't an easy decision," I said.

"He told you that, did he?" The vampire pirate nodded sagely. "He's a standup werewolf, that one."

I shot him a quizzical look. "What do you mean? Why would he tell me it wasn't an easy decision when *I* broke up with *him?*"

Captain Yellowjacket gave me a sympathetic pat on the shoulder. "It's quite all right, lassie. It happens to everyone."

"I'm willing to be broken up with, but it didn't happen," I said.

Bittersteel, the blue and red parrot that kept Captain Yellowjacket company, blew past me to rest on his perch behind the bar. "He broke up with you," the bird taunted.

"Listen," I said, my gaze fixed on Bittersteel, "I've had my fill of feathered friends this week, got it?"

Captain Yellowjacket whistled. "Well, somebody is having a hard time adjusting to the new normal."

I covered my face with my hands. "Who told you the sheriff broke up with me?"

Captain Yellowjacket craned his neck to consult the parrot. "Who was it? Wyatt?"

I rolled my eyes. Of course it was. "You know what? It's

fine." I waved my hand dismissively. I didn't need everyone in town to know it was me. I had nothing to prove. Honestly, I owed it to Sheriff Nash to let the rumor run its course.

The vampire pirate cleaned a glass and set it on the counter. "What can I get for you?"

"Ale on tap is fine," I said. "While I'm here, I want to ask about customers you had a few nights ago. A werewolf named Nola and a fairy."

The vampire pirate's pleasant expression faded. "Tatiana."

"You know her?" I queried.

"Who didn't?" He leaned over the counter and whispered, "I heard about what happened to her. Can't say I'm surprised."

"No one seems to be," I said. "How did she and Nola seem to be getting along?"

"Two oysters in a shell," he said. "Very cozy. The werewolf seemed crestfallen when the fairy decided to leave."

That seemed to correspond to what Nola told me. "Did anything noteworthy happen the night she was here?"

He scratched his beard. "She charmed the feathers off Bittersteel, which is a rare sight indeed." He laughed. "One was as inappropriate as the other. A match if I ever saw one."

"I can't believe she's gone," the parrot squawked sadly. "If ever a woman was meant to get a taste of Bittersteel…"

Captain Yellowjacket held up a hand. "All right there, friend. You can stop there."

A kiss on the curve of my neck alerted me to Alec's arrival. "Good evening, Miss Rose."

"Well, if you're going to greet her like that, I think you should be on a first name basis." Captain Yellowjacket clearly hadn't heard the news about Alec. Wyatt must've kept that part to himself.

Alec grinned. "I'm still getting accustomed to calling her Ember."

"An ale for you, Mr. Hale?"

"Yes, thank you." Alec cocked his head. "And how was your day?"

"Oh, you know. Spent a little quality time with my familiar at the dump. The usual. How was yours?"

"I finished another chapter of my novel," he said.

"Good job." I smiled at him so hard that my cheeks hurt. "Can you believe we're actually doing this?" I gestured between us. "This feels so normal already. I love it."

"I feel rather invigorated myself."

"Me-ow," the guy next to me said in a suggestive manner. I turned and followed his gaze to a sexy woman in a leopard print dress that barely covered her bottom. She wore glasses in the shape of a cat's eye.

"She looks familiar," I said.

Alec peered at her behind my back. "I can't say the same. A wereleopard, I'd wager."

I snapped my fingers. "She's the receptionist from the marketing agency where Dana Ellsworth works."

"Dana," Alec repeated. "So strange to hear her name again after so much time."

The guy next to me held up a glass of ale as an offering to the receptionist.

She sauntered over and placed a hand on his shoulder. "For me?" she practically purred. "The name's Kitty."

Of course it was.

Her eyes widened slightly when she noticed me. "Oh, I've met you. You were with the leprechaun."

"I wasn't *with* him," I said. "I just stood beside him."

Alec laughed. "Someone's touchy. What do you have against leprechauns?"

A group of leprechauns in a corner booth all lifted their heads at once.

"Nothing, nothing." I blew them kisses. "I love leprechauns, just not the one I was with."

"I guess you came to see Dana at the right time," Kitty said. "She'll be gone as of next week."

"Gone?" I said. "She quit?"

"She got a new job," Kitty said. "Frankly, half the office is relieved. She wasn't very nice and she'd been taking a lot of time off to do interviews. Of course, we didn't know she was interviewing at the time. The boss found out that she had her assistant falsifying her attendance records to make it look like she was in the office."

The gears in my mind began clicking. "How recently did this happen? What about last Monday? We were told Dana was in the office all day."

"Hey," the guy next to me said. "I bought her a drink so that I could talk to her, not you."

"This is important," I said.

"You're a chick. Nothing you have to say is that important," the guy said.

Alec made a threatening noise beside me.

"I can handle this," I said over my shoulder.

The wereleopard's arm shot out and knocked the guy straight off the stool. He landed on the floor with a thud. She smiled demurely at him. "Thanks for the drink."

"Apparently, she can handle this," I told Alec.

Kitty took the guy's spot on the stool and he scrambled away, swearing as he went. "Anyhoo, Dana was out for at least two hours on Monday. I distinctly remember because it was Sabrina's birthday and we had cake upstairs in the fishbowl. Dana never misses out on cake. It was Red Velvet."

"She lied," I said under my breath. But no, the examiner found werewolf fur on Tatiana's wings. There was no evidence of a vampire's involvement.

"Why would she lie to you about the fact that she was on a job interview?" Kitty asked.

"Because she wasn't on a job interview," I said.

She pushed her glasses back to the bridge of her nose. "She wasn't?"

I whipped around and looked at Alec. "I'm sorry to leave already, but I need to go talk to someone." Several thoughts were fighting for space in my head. Meadow's aunt and uncle. The mysterious inheritance. I was close to a breakthrough. I could feel it. I had to get downtown.

Alec slid off the stool. "I'll join you."

"No, I don't think you should," I said.

"I've been ruled out as a suspect," he said.

I placed a firm hand on his chest. Sweet baby Elvis, that was one nice chest. "Still, I don't want the appearance of impropriety."

"I'll keep your boyfriend company," the wereleopard said with a flirtatious smile.

"Thank you," I said.

She looked at me with surprise. "That's not usually how the woman responds in this situation."

I shrugged. "It took a lot for us to get to this point. I'm not worried about him."

Alec reached for me. In the blink of an eye, I was in his arms. He kissed me deeply before releasing me. "Call me if you need me. I won't hesitate to come."

The wereleopard sighed. "Why are all the good ones taken?" She guzzled down the ale, despondent.

The parrot flapped his wings and squawked. "I've got a good one right here."

I groaned. "Okay then. That's my cue to leave." I grabbed my handbag and raced out of the Whitethorn. If my theory was right, I'd have a killer behind bars before the night was over.

CHAPTER SEVENTEEN

THE FITNESS CENTER appeared dark from the outside. There was no sign of activity, but I'd passed Jake's truck in the parking lot. He had to be here.

Slowly, I pushed open the door and slipped inside. I didn't want to give him any warning. My plan was to pepper him with questions until he broke. I felt my wand poke me in the back and it gave me comfort. Jake was stronger than me in both human and wolf form. If he decided to resort to violence, I had to be ready to defend myself with magic.

At the back of the building, a light glowed. Jake's office. Bingo.

I crept down the small corridor and peered inside. I snapped back, unprepared for what I saw.

Jake was sprawled across the desk with Dana writhing on top of him. Thankfully, they were both fully clothed. Or mostly clothed. Jake's shirt was missing and I took note of Dana's bra hanging from a rafter.

Seeing them together helped the final pieces of the puzzle click into place. I tried to back out of the office as quietly as possible, so that I could alert the sheriff and Deputy Bolan to my discovery. Walking backward was not my specialty, however, and I managed to catch my heel and trip. I landed squarely on my bottom and swallowed my cry when my tail-bone hit the floor.

"What was that noise?" Dana asked.

Stupid vampire hearing!

Dana poked her head out of the office. "What are you doing here?" she asked when she spotted me on the floor. Her voice sparked with anger and suspicion.

I scrambled backward like a crab. "I came to see Jake, but I can see he's busy, so I wanted to show myself out."

Dana gave her boyfriend a menacing look. "Are you cheating on me again, you filthy animal?"

Jake appeared in the corridor. "No, baby. Of course not."

"I wanted to set up personal training sessions with Jake," I lied.

Dana eyed me carefully. "How personal?" She turned to Jake. "I am not going to marry you if you keep this up. I can't constantly wonder about you when you're not with me."

Jake held up his hands. "I swear, baby. There's no one else. There never has been. You know that."

I tried to rise to my feet, but Dana was too quick for me. Stupid vampire speed! She was beside me in a nanosecond, her foot pressing hard on my stomach.

"Don't move," the vampire said. "You look familiar."

Jake came over to examine me. "She's the one asking about Tatiana." They exchanged looks of alarm, the realization settling in.

"The investigation is over," I lied. The tip of my wand dug into my back. I had to reach it somehow, but Dana was too fast for me, especially when she was practically on top of me.

The vampire studied me. "Over? You caught the killer?"

"Yes," I said. "A werewolf named Nola."

Dana didn't remove her foot from my stomach, but she

appeared to take the news in stride. "Thank the devil. It's about time justice was served. Isn't that right, Jake?"

"Absolutely," the werewolf said. "I can't believe it was one of my own."

"She's an Arctic wolf," I said. "Not quite your pack." I gestured to Dana's foot. "Would you mind removing your foot? I'd like to stand." And leave. Quickly.

Dana lifted her foot, but I sensed her hesitation. "Why can't I read your mind?" she asked.

I hopped to my feet and took a step backward. "My boyfriend is a vampire. Alec Hale."

Dana's eyes flickered with recognition. I figured if she knew Alec was my boyfriend that she'd be less inclined to— you know—kill me.

"Can you teach me how to do that?" Jake asked.

Dana shot him an annoyed look. "So you can lie to me, Jake? I don't think so. We're not going to start our lives as husband and wife with secrets."

"How about I leave you two to enjoy your special time?" I said. "Sorry to interrupt. Jake, we can discuss training another time."

Dana studied me. "Why are you so nervous?"

"Because you're a vampire with an anger management issue," I said. "And you just accused me of cheating with your boyfriend."

Dana scrutinized me. "Tell me. How did Nola kill Tatiana?"

"According to the evidence, Nola knocked her on the head and threw her in the pool where she drowned," I replied. "We found werewolf fur, too."

"That's right," Jake said. A look of confusion crossed his face. "And the evidence matched Nola's?"

Dana swiveled toward her boyfriend and smacked him in

the stomach. "Of course it matches Nola's, idiot. She's the killer."

"I'm glad that's cleared up," I said. "I'll see you around." I took a step backward.

"It's probably best that you don't tell anyone about Jake and me. We're trying to keep our relationship low-key in light of Tatiana's unfortunate passing."

"We're getting married," Jake said.

I thought Dana was going to sink her teeth into his neck until it snapped. "Shut up, Jake," she said.

"What?" Jake's expression was pure innocence. "What does it matter if everyone knows now? Tatiana is dead and they arrested Nola. We're not suspects anymore, which means we can leave town and start our life together." He hooked his arm around Dana's waist. "I can't wait to shout it from the rooftops. Dana Ellsworth and Jake Goode are finally getting married!"

"Good luck to both of you," I said, and turned to leave. I now had enough information to have them both arrested. I just needed to alert Deputy Bolan.

"Hey, I told you when you interviewed me that I was leaving town as soon as the investigation was over," Jake said. "If you know Nola's the killer, why would you come to me now to start personal training?"

I froze in my tracks and swiveled around. "I thought you might be able to set me up with a daily routine before you go. I mean, you're the best in town, right?"

"Of course I am." He stood perfectly erect, soaking up the admiration.

Dana rolled her eyes. "Are you that much of a moron, Jake? Apparently, a woman doesn't need magic to pull one over on you. A little ego stroke and…"

I didn't wait around to hear the rest. Instead, I bolted for the door.

I heard the snarl behind me and whipped around with my wand in my hand. "*Glaciare!*" I turned quickly and aimed too high. I missed the wolf completely, covering a picture on the wall in a sheen of ice instead.

He surged forward and I ran. I threaded my way through the row of elliptical machines and climbed up onto the seat of a stationary bicycle so that I could grab one of the ribbons that hung from the ceiling. I shimmied to the top to stay out of reach. The wolf jumped and snapped his jaws. I swung forward and caught the next ribbon, then tucked my legs under me—not as easy as it sounds when hanging from the ceiling.

Dana's fangs glimmered in the dim light. I had to make another move. The vampire could easily vault from a piece of equipment and grab me. With my fingers curled tightly around the ribbon, I maneuvered my wand to point at Dana. The way she was looking at me made the back of my neck prickle. Her expression was cold and calculating.

"You can't kill me," I said. "Then the sheriff will know it was you. That you were covering your tracks with Tatiana."

Dana folded her arms. "How ironic would it be if both girlfriends of Alec Hale and Sheriff Nash were murdered in the same week?"

The large wolf watched with angry eyes as I swayed overhead.

"Tatiana manipulated them," I said. "Just like she did to Jake. You're all victims of Tatiana's treachery." Of course, that didn't give anyone carte blanche to kill her.

"She was supposed to be my best friend and she destroyed my relationship with Jake. For fun. I wasted years being bitter and angry with him. I should have believed him when he first told me." She cast a glance at the wolf. "I guess I needed a few years to thaw out."

The wolf howled.

"I know, baby." She turned back to me. "When Jake suggested luring her back here, I was all for it. Tatiana didn't deserve to live. All she did was spread misery and pain. She was a disease that needed to be eradicated."

My arms began to ache and my hands grew slick with sweat. I wouldn't be able to dangle much longer. A variety of spells ran through my mind. I had to tackle Dana first, then Jake. She was the bigger threat while I was up here.

"Come down," Dana said. "Don't make this harder on yourself than it has to be."

"I'm not making it harder for me," I said. "I'm making it harder for you." And then I realized what would make it even harder.

I released my wand-free hand from the ribbon and reached into my pocket. Pain radiated down my other arm as I fought to hold on. I closed my hand around the small draw-string bag inside and began to chant in Latin.

Dana saw I was up to something. She ran to the nearest elliptical machine to launch herself at the ribbon. She leaped into the air just as I disappeared. She swiped at the empty air and missed, dropping to the floor. Thankfully, she was too consumed by confusion and rage to notice the swinging motion of the neighboring ribbon—the one I'd grabbed in my invisible state.

"What in the devil's name?" Dana said. She stood beneath me, hands on hips. Her head swiveled, trying to understand what happened. "Can that witch teleport?"

I gripped the ribbon with both hands and tried to stay motionless. The spell wouldn't last forever. I had to sneak out before I reappeared.

The wolf sniffed the air and growled. *Crap on a stick.* Jake could smell that I was still here. At least he was on the floor.

I waited until Dana turned her head again and oh-so-carefully reached for the next ribbon. The closer I could get to the exit, the better.

"Jake, find her trail and track her," Dana ordered. "We have to stop her before she gets to the sheriff."

The wolf circled below me, trying to locate my scent. I had to make another move. My heart was hammering so hard and fast that I was sure they could both hear it. I reached for the next ribbon and, thanks to the wand I still clutched in my hand, my fingers failed to make it all the way around the material. I fell to the floor, albeit still invisible.

The wolf whipped toward me and growled. Although I knew he couldn't see me, he could sense my presence.

"You smell her, Jake?" Dana squinted in my direction, but she was slightly off the mark.

I backed away slowly, trying to reach the door. Only a few more steps.

Dana's lips curled into a cruel smile at the same time my body stopped tingling. "Going somewhere?" she asked sweetly.

The wolf lunged and I raced for the door. Sharp nails sliced my back and I cried out in pain. I felt the blood seeping from the wound. I fell into the door and pushed it open with my body, spilling onto the walkway. I flipped onto my bottom, ignoring the pain, and kicked the door closed before my attackers had a chance to follow me outside.

I summoned my will and pointed my wand at the door. "*Glaciare*!" Ice covered the door and sealed it shut. I couldn't believe I remembered that spell. The last time I'd used it was to save Cephas. Actually, that wasn't strictly true. I'd used it chill a bottle of white wine a few weeks ago, when I was too lazy to stick it in the freezer for a couple of hours. Magic had its perks.

Dana pounded on the door, vowing to tear me into pieces. I dragged myself to my feet and pulled out my phone to call for help. It wouldn't take Dana and Jake long to break through one of the side windows.

Before I finished dialing, lights flashed behind me. I spun around to see the sheriff's car pulling into the parking lot. Sheriff Nash shot out of the car like it was on fire.

"Go around the side before they leave through the window," I yelled. Between the invisibility spell and the ice spell, I was too drained of energy to perform any more magic.

The sheriff disappeared around the corner of the building and emerged a few minutes later, appearing satisfied. "They're both down. I'll just need to transport them."

"Down?" I echoed. "How did you manage that?"

He patted his jacket. "Tranquilizer gun."

I finally relaxed. "How did you know to come here?" I asked.

The sheriff refused to meet my gaze. "I saw unusual activity and decided to check it out."

I closed my eyes, the realization setting in. "You were *patrolling* again, weren't you?"

He raked a hand through his dark hair. "You know I worry about you, Rose. Without knowing the who or why of Tatiana's death, I was concerned that you might be a target."

"You don't need to worry about me," I said. "It's not your job."

He didn't get a chance to argue because Deputy Bolan pulled into the parking lot, his siren blaring. "I'm here!" He hopped out of the car without even bothering to close the door. "What happened?"

"Jake and Dana," I said. "They were in cahoots this whole time. They lured Tatiana here with the promise of a fake inheritance and then killed her. My guess is Dana hit her in the head with the chair and then Jake pushed her in the pool in his wolf form. That's why his fur was stuck to her wings."

Deputy Bolan's expression darkened. "Revenge is an ugly business."

"You should take another sample of Jake's fur while he's still in wolf form," I said. "It'll match what was found at the crime scene."

"I'm surprised he actually gave a sample the first time," the deputy said. "He had to know it would be a match."

"Did he bring the sample or did you have him turn and take it from him at the office?" Sheriff Nash asked.

Ohhhh. "He didn't submit a sample of his own fur, did he?"

"Doubtful," the sheriff said.

So even if the lab hadn't botched the samples, they wouldn't have found a match. Jake was smarter than he appeared.

"I bet it was Dana's idea," the sheriff said. "There was a reason she and Tatiana were friends before the fallout over Jake. Cunning doesn't begin to describe them."

Hmm, good point. I gave Jake too much credit.

"I wasn't there when Jake brought in his sample," Deputy Bolan said. "I guess we'll need to review protocol with everyone in the office."

The sheriff hooked his thumbs through the belt loops of his tight jeans. "Good idea, but I've got to accept responsibility, too. If I'd been more involved, I could've prevented it."

"You couldn't have been more involved," I protested. "It wouldn't have looked good."

"Since when do I care about that, Rose?" he said. "This is my town and crime here is my responsibility."

"Do you need help getting them into the car?" I asked.

"We'll take it from here," the sheriff said. "You can come by the office tomorrow morning to give me the full story. Right now you should go see a healer to take care of those cuts on your back."

The mention of the claw marks made me wince as my brain registered the pain once more. "Yeah, you're right. They're starting to burn."

"You take care of yourself, Rose," the sheriff said.

"I always do," I said. If there was one thing I'd learned in my crazy life, it was how to survive.

CHAPTER EIGHTEEN

THE NEXT MORNING I dropped off Marley at the academy and headed straight to the sheriff's office to give my report. His door was open, so I knocked on the wooden frame. "Good morning."

His head jerked up. "Hey, Rose. How's your back?"

"Better," I said. Marley had been asleep when I arrived home and Mrs. Babcock had insisted on taking care of my wounds herself. The brownie was like Mary Poppins without the umbrella.

He waved me forward. "Come and sit. I promise I won't bite."

I entered the office and plopped down in the chair opposite his desk. "Paperwork?" I asked, noting the scattered pages on his desk.

"Yep. Got a heap of it now that Jake and Dana have been apprehended." He wore a vague smile. "Thanks for that, by the way."

"Anything for you," I replied.

His expression turned sad. "Not anything, Rose." He shook his head, as though silently chastising himself.

"How'd you figure out it was them? Deputy Bolan and I were talking about it last night and couldn't put it together."

"It was only last night when we ran into Kitty, the receptionist from Dana's office, that all the pieces clicked into place."

"We?"

I swore in my head. "Alec and I were at the Whitethorn for a drink."

His jaw tensed. "Got it."

"Kitty mentioned that Dana had quit and was taking a new job. Jake had also mentioned moving out of Starry Hollow to somewhere far away. The timing was too suspect. Then I remembered a story Bentley had told me about his fiancée's aunt and uncle."

His brow creased. "The elf in your office? What do they have to do with Jake and Dana?"

"They'd been married and then had a bitter divorce, and now they're back together. Their story made me think of Jake and Dana. I wanted to go back and talk to Jake again and test my theory."

He inclined his head, curious. "Which was?"

"That they'd quietly reunited at some point, but only pretended to hate each other until the investigation was over. Then they planned to leave town and start a new life together."

The sheriff scribbled a few notes. "So they showed up at Tanya's house together to kill Tatiana." The sheriff set down his pen and rubbed the back of his head. "The couple that kills together, stays together, I guess."

"They both hated Tatiana for ruining their relationship."

"Funny how there are different reactions to similar behavior," the sheriff said.

"How do you mean?"

"I never hated Tatiana for what she did. I felt sorry for her."

I ran my hands along the arms of the chair—a nervous gesture because I was...well, nervous. "Before I go, I just want to apologize."

"For?"

"Everything," I blurted. "Having to treat you like a suspect. Bolan and I didn't want to, but neither one of us wanted to turn the investigation over to that other sheriff either. He hates you too much."

"I know and I appreciate that," he said. "Not saying I liked the situation, but I understood." He tapped the pen on the desk. "As far as everything else goes, you already apologized about a thousand times. You don't need to keep doing it."

I nodded. "How are you feeling about Tatiana?" I asked. "You must have mixed feelings about her death."

"I can't say I'll miss her, but I never wanted her dead, no matter how awful she was."

"Oh, I know that," I said. "But you knew her well and..."

He scoffed. "Nobody knew Tatiana well, Rose. That fairy made sure of it. She had no interest in being genuine or kind or any of the traits that make us vulnerable to another living creature."

"Still," I said, "she'd been an important part of your life, however briefly." Once upon a time, Tatiana had meant something to him. Part of him had to be grieving, whether he acknowledged it or not.

The sheriff returned his attention to the papers on his desk. "Is that it, Rose? Because I have a lot of work to do now that I'm back in the helm."

I thumped my thumb on the arm of the chair. "I'm not good with this sort of thing. You know that."

"Apologies?"

"Speaking from the heart," I said. "My heart."

"I'm guessing you and Hale are going to have some awfully quiet counseling sessions."

My stomach jolted. "You know about that? Exactly how much of your day involves stalking me?"

"Heck, half the town knows about it," he said. "The two of you are minor celebrities, don't forget. The elusive vampire writer and a descendant of the One True Witch. Residents are interested."

"I want to start off our relationship on the right foot," I said.

"Maybe I should have suggested counseling from the get-go," he said. "Maybe that was my first mistake."

My throat went dry. "Your *first* mistake? You think of me as a mistake?"

His expression softened. "No, gods no. Of course not. I didn't mean it like that, Rose. I just wish I could've done something differently, so that you would think of me the way you think of him."

I drew my knees to my chest. I wanted to curl up in a ball and weep. "I'm so sorry, Granger. I wish that for you, too."

"But not for you," he said.

"How much do you hate me?" I whispered. "Is it an all-consuming hatred or a low hum of hatred that's more like background noise?"

He stared at me intently. "If I didn't hate Tatiana, do you seriously think I'd hate you? Don't ever think that, Rose. I swear to you it's not possible."

Tears slid down my cheeks. "Why not? I'd hate me. I've been so unfair to you."

He got up from the chair behind the desk and moved to sit in the seat next to mine. His hand covered mine. "Listen to me because I want to be perfectly clear about this. I do not hate you. I will never hate you. I love you too much for that."

My chest tightened. He loved me and I'd treated him like

a toy to be discarded when a shinier one came along. "I don't deserve your love."

He squeezed my hand. "Well, tough, because it's yours whether you think you deserve it or not. I'm not going to stop loving you because you don't feel the same, Rose. Real love doesn't work that way. It settles into your bones. Becomes a part of who you are."

I wholeheartedly agreed with that. I'd continued to love Alec even when I thought he felt nothing for me. It hurt like hell, but my feelings didn't stop.

"While you and Hale are working on your relationship, I'll be working on myself," the sheriff said. "My goal is to get to the place where I can love you without expecting or hoping for something in return. I don't know if I can do it, but I'm determined to try."

I sniffed and nodded. "I do want to be friends, Granger."

"And I'd like that, too, but I warn you, it might take time." He released my hand. "I'm not perfect, Rose. I can't just snap into whatever form you want me in now. My heart needs time to heal, to catch up with my head."

Great balls of heartache, I hated myself for hurting him. "You deserve so much better than what I've given you."

"Maybe one day the universe will agree with you," he said. "So far, it's been kind of a losing streak."

I exhaled softly. "You're amazing, do you know that?"

"I know, and so are you." His mouth warmed to a grin. "We'll get through this, you and me."

I pushed myself to my feet. "I'm glad you think so. I don't tend to have a lot of faith in general."

"Then I'll have enough for the both of us."

"Have a good day, Granger." Instinctively, I bent to kiss his cheek, but then thought better of it and straightened.

He stared at his desk, pretending not to notice. "You, too, Rose."

. . .

Marley stood in the front garden of the cottage, aiming her wand at the roses. PP3 waited patiently by her feet and I wondered what was going through his terrier mind. Did he think she was about to produce dog treats on the bushes?

I peered over her shoulder. "Which spell are you practicing?"

Marley jumped. "Mom! Don't sneak up on me like that." She craned her neck to give me a disapproving look.

"I wasn't sneaking," I said. "I walked out the front door. Didn't even bother to tiptoe."

She turned back to the roses. "I guess I was concentrating so hard that I didn't hear you."

"What's your goal?" I asked, stepping beside her.

"I want to change the roses into tulips."

"And you know the spell for that?" I asked.

She licked her lips. "Yes, I found it in the grimoire that Aunt Hyacinth gave me."

"Maybe you should stick to spells you're learning at the academy for now," I suggested.

Marley eyed me. "Are you trying to stifle my growth?"

I laughed. "No, Marley. I'm trying to make sure you don't wipe out all the roses and incur Aunt Hyacinth's wrath."

"She's the one who gave me the grimoire," Marley said. "I would think she'd be happy I'm trying to excel."

I placed a hand on her arm. "Just take your time, Marley. I know you're smart and capable, but you're only eleven. There's no rush."

A car appeared in the distance and my heart skipped a beat when I recognized Alec's sleek black sedan.

Marley brightened at the sight. "Is Alec coming for dinner?" she asked hopefully.

"Maybe?" I replied. If so, I had to figure out how to cook something quickly that didn't burn. *Ha! Good luck, Ember.*

Marley seemed to forget about her spell and ran to greet the vampire. He emerged from the car holding a large container. "Good evening to my two favorite witches."

"What's in the container?" Marley asked. She inhaled deeply. "It smells delicious."

"I hope you don't mind, but I took the liberty of ordering one of my favorite meals from La Cucina," he said. "I thought the three of us could have dinner together to celebrate solving Tatiana's murder."

PP3 barked his approval.

I think he means the four of us. Raoul appeared from around the corner of the cottage. No doubt the aroma reached his hiding spot.

"Ah, your bandit friend," Alec said, his gaze alighting on the raccoon. "I suppose he'll be joining us."

Raoul scampered over. *Food and a decent nickname? Have I mentioned how much I like this guy?*

Bonkers flew to Marley's shoulder, seemingly out of thin air. The winged cat must have also sensed the arrival of food. It was like living with a house full of teenagers.

"I'll take this inside," Marley said, and accepted the container from Alec. The animals trailed behind her like she was the Pied Piper of Hamelin.

I stood on my toes and gave Alec a kiss on the cheek. "This is a nice surprise. Thank you."

"No, thank *you*," the vampire said. "You kept your head and were able to figure out what really happened to Tatiana. As deplorable as she was, she deserves justice."

"I'm glad you feel that way," I said. In a way, he and Sheriff Nash were more similar than they realized.

He looked into my eyes. "Were you afraid I wouldn't? That I possess the ruthlessness of a vampire like Dana?"

"No, but I understand how hard it is to let go of strong emotions," I said. "That even when you desperately want to let go, you can't quite manage it."

He circled an arm around my waist and pulled me closer. "I don't want to let go, Ember. Not this time."

I smiled. "Good, because neither do I."

* * *

Thanks for reading! Sign up for my cozy newsletter and receive a FREE short story that introduces Raoul and Ember: http://eepurl.com/ctYNzf

ALSO BY ANNABEL CHASE

Spellbound

Curse the Day, Book 1

Doom and Broom, Book 2

Spell's Bells, Book 3

Lucky Charm, Book 4

Better Than Hex, Book 5

Cast Away, Book 6

A Touch of Magic, Book 7

A Drop in the Potion, Book 8

Hemlocked and Loaded, Book 9

All Spell Breaks Loose, Book 10

Spellbound Ever After

Crazy For Brew, Book 1

Lost That Coven Feeling, Book 2

Wands Upon A Time, Book 3

Spellslingers Academy of Magic

Outcast, Warden of the West, Book 1

Outclassed, Warden of the West, Book 2

Outlast, Warden of the West, Book 3

Outlier, Sentry of the South, Book 1

Outfox, Sentry of the South, Book 2

Outbreak, Sentry of the South, Book 3

Outwit, Enforcer of the East, Book 1
Outlaw, Enforcer of the East, Book 2

Outrun, Keeper of the North, Book 1
Outgrow, Keeper of the North, Book 2